Caged

A Twisted Fairy Tale

Lena Mae Hill

Caged
Copyright © 2019 Lena Mae Hill

Dedication

For the readers who asked for this book.

Table of Contents

Chapter One

Astrid

I stood before the mirror wrestling to get the whalebone comb through my hair. My mother had given it to me for my twelfth birthday, reminding me that it came from the sea itself, and aside from me, it was her most treasured possession. Too bad I couldn't enchant it with magical detangling properties. I'd asked, but Mother Dear said I had so little magic that I couldn't afford to waste it on frivolous things.

I'd looked up the word frivolous in my battered dictionary after she'd left, and I didn't think combing my ridiculous hair was frivolous. It was a safety precaution.

As I thought of her, her voice drifted down to me.

"Astrid…"

I dropped the comb onto my vanity table and raced to the ladder, slipping and sliding on the piles of gold droplets scattered across the floor. Pitching forward, I grabbed onto the ladder and hugged it for dear life, my feet having gone out from under me. When I'd scrabbled my feet until I found the solid floor beneath the mess, I scampered up the ladder. I'd forgotten to close the trap door, and Mother Dear would be angry if she caught it standing open yet again.

I boosted myself over the lip of the opening and onto the floor of my main room. Biting my lip and scrunching my face in concentration, I lowered the door, willing it to be quiet so she wouldn't hear it close. It gave a little squeak, and my heart lurched. I hurriedly rolled the rug back over the door and ran to the window.

"Where have you been?" Mother Dear demanded. "I've been waiting for ten minutes. It's freezing out here. Lower the basket."

"Sorry, sorry," I said, lifting the large, hand-woven basket off its hook near the window. I checked the knot as I did every time, and when I was sure it was secure, I began to lower it to where Mother Dear waited far below, an old woman lying on the ground at her feet.

When the basket reached her, Mother Dear gathered up the body and heaved it in.

"Haul her up," she called, and I began to pull the rope, going hand over hand and being careful to move smoothly so I didn't bang the load against the wall. Mother Dear didn't like when I did that. It caused bruising.

When the basket arrived at the window, I looped the rope around the hook and reached out to grab the load and pull it in. I'd woven the basket entirely out of my own hair, and it was soft and pliable, if a bit scratchy. After setting it gently on the floor, I opened it to reveal the body of a plump, wrinkled person.

"Oh," I gasped, kneeling beside her. Swallowing hard, I reached out a trembling hand. My fingers with their tight, young skin touched the softest skin I'd ever seen. I didn't know what had happened to the woman. Her face had been worn thin and crumpled up like an old sheet of paper that had been hidden away in a hurry too many times, only to be retrieved and smoothed out again when one's mother was far away. The corners of her mouth sagged down like she'd been sad when she was crumpled up and stowed in a secret place.

"Astrid," Mother Dear barked from outside. "The basket?"

"Sorry," I said, jumping to my feet and yanking it free of the wrinkled woman. "Sorry!" I tossed the basket out, letting it fall all the way down. Mother Dear stepped in and settled herself, and I began to draw her up. Hand over hand, my muscles flexing and my hands tiring by the time Mother Dear had reached the window. She pulled herself in, climbing out of the basket and brushing herself off.

"You'd think by now you could remember how this works," Mother Dear said. "Do you expect me to fly up here? Climb the wall with my bare hands? Even you can't be that stupid."

I crouched beside the woman and poked her soft face with one finger. "What happened to her?"

"She got old, that's what," Mother Dear said, unwinding her scarf and shaking out her long blonde hair.

"That's what a person with oldness looks like?" I asked, staring at the woman. Mother Dear was terrified of the disease she called *oldness*, so she put spells on to make herself look young. I had never seen old before.

"Now you understand why I don't want to look like this hideous old hag," Mother Dear said. "What man would want me then? Youth and beauty are the only things they like more than treasure. If you don't have those, you're worth less than a dog to them."

I examined the woman more closely. I hadn't thought she was hideous. She looked different than the young bodies mother sometimes inhabited, yes, but not unpleasant. Mother Dear was the most beautiful person in the world. She always told me that. I was next, she said, but I couldn't be prettiest because my hair was a bright auburn instead of pale gold like hers. Sometimes, though, Mother Dear had to use other people as disguises. I didn't know what that would be like. I always looked the same, as I had nowhere to go and no one to see me in disguise.

"How long will you be here?" I asked Mother Dear. "Can you stay a few days?"

"Oh, darling, I wish I could."

"If you wish you could, then why don't you?"

"We can't just do anything we want," Mother Dear said.

"Why not?"

"Because that's not the way the world works," she said. "We can't just do whatever feels good or take whatever we see."

I didn't see why. If it felt good, why wouldn't we want to do it? And Mother Dear took whatever she wanted. She took my treasure to buy things. She even took other people's bodies when she needed them.

"These few days are the most important days of our lives," she said, leaving the body in front of the window and sinking onto the edge of the bed.

"What do you mean?" I asked.

She patted the space beside her, and after a moment I joined her. We sat on the edge of the bed, our knees angled toward each other as she took my hands in hers. "My precious daughter," she said, smiling and stroking my hair behind my ear.

"What is it, Mother Dear?" I asked, my heart suddenly beating right against the bottom of my throat.

Her fingers tangled, and she had to shake her them loose. "This is the moment we've been waiting for our whole lives."

"It is?"

"Yes," she said. "I've been waiting for this since before you were even born, my dearest daughter. The next few days will set up our whole lives, giving us all we've ever dreamed of."

I closed my eyes and took a breath, letting hope spread its wings like a bird inside my chest. Everything I'd dreamed of. Running down the mountainside below the tower where I'd lived for all sixteen years of my life. Flying out the window and over the valleys filled with puffy treetops below and puffy clouds above. Visiting my father, who I'd only met a handful of times, telling him I was no better than his other daughters, that I didn't have to be hidden away like the treasure downstairs that he and my mother hoarded like dragons in the fairytales on my bookshelf.

"Will I be able to go outside?" I asked, my lips stiff with hoping so hard.

"Yes," Mother Dear said.

"Out there?" I gasped. Adrenaline raced from my adrenal glands and through my bloodstream, racing along the highways of veins that delivered it to my limbs. That's how it happened. I'd read about it in the encyclopedia on my shelf.

"Well, you can't very well marry the prince up here in your tower," Mother Dear said.

"Marry the prince?" I squeaked. Of course, that was my destiny. My mother had told me. It was in all the stories. It was a good thing, what every princess wanted. So, it must be what I wanted. That must be the feeling in my stomach like I'd eaten bad meat.

"There's a lot to do down in the valley," Mother Dear said, squeezing my hands. "I have to go back tonight. I'll come for you soon, my dear."

"And I can go with you then? I can see my father again?"

"Of course, darling. He will teach you how to rule the Third Valley after he's gone. Until then, you'll rule the Second Valley with the wolf king as your husband."

"But...I don't know how to rule werewolves."

"Oh, don't worry. You don't have to be strong or smart to do that. You just tell me everything, and I'll tell you what's best."

"And I'll meet my sisters," I said, clasping my hands at the thought.

"Defeat your evil sisters," Mother Dear corrected.

"Sorry, sorry," I said. "Defeat my sisters and marry the prince."

"And live happily ever after," she said, enunciating each word and giving my cheek a pat with each one.

"Okay," I breathed. "I'm ready."

"You're playing your part," she said. "For my part, I'll need a disguise for the night. I'll be back tomorrow or the next day. So much is at stake, Astrid. I'm setting it all in motion." She rose from the bed, her voice rising in power. She held out both arms, throwing her head back as she faced the window. "My plans have all come together. It all depends on this. Everything comes together at the eclipse."

"There's an eclipse?" I asked, shivering. The first time I'd seen one, I thought the moon had died and lay bleeding in the sky.

"In just a few days," she said, nudging me off my bed. "That's when we claim our destiny." She scooted under the blanket and lay on her back, as she always did. A moment later, her body went still. I stood over her reciting the chant she had taught me as a child, the one that kept anyone from inhabiting her body when she took over someone else's. Not everyone could wear different bodies like she did, but just in case, I had to keep her protected.

Before I'd even finished the spell, Mother Dear stood up wearing the body of the old woman. She could move from one body to another, a fact that she was quite proud of. Almost no one possessed this skill. She could never fool me, though. Over the years, I had learned how to spot her in whatever disguise she wore. After all, she was the only human I had to study, so I had taught myself everything about her, memorizing her the way I did the books on my shelves.

"Come lower me down," she said, stepping into the basket.

I stood up from the bed, forgetting that I'd left my hair loose, and promptly stepped on it. I lurched to that side, hopping on one foot to keep my balance.

"Oh, for the love of Thalassa," Mother Dear snapped, yanking the rope free of the hook. I made it to her side, my eyes watering from the sting of pulled hair. This was why a comb was not frivolous. My hair was going to be the death of me if I didn't watch out. If it wasn't attached to my head, I would have sworn it was out to get me.

"Sorry, sorry," I muttered, grabbing the rope and looping it over the bar that served as our pulley system. Mother Dear scooted onto the windowsill on her bottom, maneuvering the basket out the window before stepping down into it. There was always a moment of sickening terror when her weight left the sill and transferred to the basket.

I tightened my grip on the rope, a knot lodging in my throat. It slowly unwound as I lowered her closer and closer to the ground and to safety. For these few minutes, I had her life in my hands. If I messed up, she would fall to her death.

And I would die here alone. No prince would come to my rescue, despite my mother's promise that I was the shifter princess, the true heir to the throne. No one would know I was here at all. The only people who knew of my existence were my mother and father. If anyone else knew, they would try to kill me. That's why Mother Dear had hidden me away for safekeeping.

People could not be trusted. They would steal me and hurt me, make me do what they wanted, take away my freedom and make me a prisoner and a slave. Or worse.

My father was the Shifter King. His wife wanted me dead so her own children could claim their throne. Luckily for me, Mother Dear had saved me as an infant and run away from all that, giving up her life to protect me. She kept me safe like a treasure, because that's what I was to her. Her treasure. One day, when she could get rid of my father's wife, I would emerge as the shifter valley's secret weapon. The real heir to the throne. But even though I held the fate of the shifter world in my hands, I didn't feel like a princess or a treasure. I just felt like me.

Mother Dear climbed out of the hair basket and gave it a tug so I'd know to pull it back up, so that no one could climb in and come to get me. That's why there were no doors in my house, no windows except this one which was far too high for anyone to enter or spot me through. But now, I leaned out the window of my tower, a lighthouse overlooking the bare winter trees of the Three Valleys.

"Bye, Mother Dear," I called. I waved until I could no longer see her borrowed body through the leafless trees. Then I turned back to the room and began the hour-long process of putting all my hair up. Sitting on the edge of the bed, I talked to Mother Dear's empty body. I liked it when she left a body for me to talk to. Even if there was no one in it, it made me feel less alone.

Chapter Two

Jack

My brothers and I stumbled into the yard, reeling against each other to stay upright. I stumbled on the steps, going to my knees before snagging the doorknob by luck alone. "Little pig, little pig, let us come in," I hollered.

My brothers burst into honks of laughter behind me. Daniel fell against the side of the trailer, which rocked and groaned on its cinderblock foundation.

The door to the trailer suddenly jerked inwards, and I tipped over, sprawling halfway through the door with my legs still hanging down the cinderblock steps. The four of us howled with laughter as Ma stood over us, her hands planted on her skinny hips.

"You think this is funny?" she demanded.

"Aww, come on, it's kinda funny," I said, rolling onto my back to look up at her.

"How many nights are you going to come home drunk and expect to live in this house, under my roof?" she asked. "How many more days am I going to have to put up with this? That's all I want to know."

"Come on, Ma, we're only kids," William said, stumbling over my body as he made his way inside. He tried to put an arm around Ma, but she shoved him away, turning her back on her useless sons.

"Kids who are old enough to get jobs instead of flushing our money down the toilet with your piss," Ma said, throwing her hands up. I saw tears in her eyes, and my laughter disappeared quicker than a bottle of the whiskey in our hands. Our father had found it hilarious to name us after the stuff, so how could we be anything but worthless drunks like him?

"I'll get a job," I said.

Evan nodded up at her from where he stood at the bottom of the steps. He lifted his foot, but he couldn't seem to find the step to put it on, so he just crumpled on top of my legs.

"You said that last week," Ma said, her shoulders shaking. "You said that last month. I don't know how else to say it. We have no money. Nothing. What are we going to eat?"

"We can eat grass," I offered. Not that it would be very satisfying for my human body, but I could live on it if I stayed in animal form for a while. One less mouth for her to feed. Considering that I wasn't even her son—Dad had washed his hands of me and Daniel when he washed his hands of her—I didn't blame her for being done with me.

"We can sell William again," Daniel said. "People pay good money for a cow."

"Not a cow," William slurred, his hands balling into fists. "I'm a bull." The two of them started punching and rolling around. William was particularly sensitive about his animal form.

"I'd sell myself if I thought any man would want me," Ma muttered.

"No way," I said as Evan slipped an arm around her slumped shoulders. "We'll take care of it. We've got you, Ma."

"Everyone in the valley knows the old cow trick," Ma said, crumpling into a chair. "Even the humans know not to buy things from us, even if they don't know where the cow disappears to in the morning."

"I'm not a cow," William growled from under Daniel, groping for his glasses, which had fallen off in the scuffle.

"What else are we going to do?" I asked. "Even if we can eat grass, you can't."

Ma dropped her head into her hands, resting her elbows on the battered table. She was a human, but for obvious reasons, she knew about shifters. Most humans in the valleys knew we weren't like regular people, though they didn't all know how. But it was kinda hard to get knocked up by a shifter and not figure it out, even if he left pretty soon after bestowing the name of his favorite drink on your sons.

"We'll go further," I said. "We'll go out of the valley. Someone in town might pay for a bull."

"How are you going to get to town?" Ma asked, rubbing her forehead.

"We'll walk."

The car had broken down months ago, and even though our mad scientist William could have fixed it, we couldn't seem to save enough money to buy the parts he needed.

"Fine," Ma said to the table. "You could use the fresh air. Don't cross through the First Valley, and don't come home until you're sober."

"We won't," I said. "We know better than to cross the witches."

"Or you," Daniel said, dismounting William and offering him a hand up.

"We'll bring you back some money," I promised.

Evan leaned down to kiss the top of her head, and I followed suit. She might not have given birth to me, but she was my mother, and I was going to make her proud. One day, I was going to do something so good she'd never be ashamed of me again.

Chapter Three

Astrid

I stood at the window, watching the red circle of shadow creep over the full moon's face. Now I knew it wasn't blood that made the moon turn red. I'd read all about eclipses in my encyclopedia.

"Where are you?" I whispered, as if the moon had the answer. I turned and paced back to the bed. Mother Dear's body lay silent and still as always. She wasn't in it. But where was she? Why hadn't she come back for me?

I paced to the window again and watched the moon hide its face. A shiver went through me, and not only because the air was damp and chilly outside my window. Something about watching this alone made me feel even more lonely, as if emphasizing that Mother Dear was not beside me. She never spent a lot of time with me, so it wasn't just that she'd been gone for a few days. She'd promised to come back before the eclipse, and she hadn't.

I pulled the basket to my side, examining the knot holding the handle, the tight weave of the hair. Maybe I could lower myself down. I pondered through how I would go about that. I'd need a lot more rope. I'd need double the rope, so I could lower myself on one and control the descent with the second rope. It was no good. I didn't have two ropes. I sighed and slid down the wall, pressing my back to the cold stone.

"Where are you?" I whispered again. The empty room had no reply.

When I woke the next morning, my shoulder was aching, and my neck cramped from sleeping on the hard floor. I sat up, blinking away sleep. "Astrid," called an impatient voice.

"Mother Dear," I cried, leaping to my feet and grabbing the basket. I tossed it down, letting the rope unwind all at once. Hand over hand, I yanked the basket up as fast as I could. As soon as the old lady disguise appeared, I tugged the basket through the window. "What happened? Why didn't you come back? I was so afraid you'd been hurt or killed or kidnapped or—"

"I don't have time for this," Mother Dear said, brushing past me and going to the bed.

"But what happened?" I asked, running to her side. "I've been waiting here all night, Mother Dear. At least tell me where you've been."

"I've been with your father," she said, lying down on the bed next to her abandoned body.

"Really?"

"Yes, darling," she said, her voice softening. She reached up a gnarled hand and caressed my cheek. "Now let me get back into my real body before I have to spend one more minute in this rotting flesh bag."

"Okay," I said, tears pooling in my eyes as I nodded and smiled and cried with relief all at once. Mother Dear left one body to enter her usual one, and a minute later, she sat up.

"Much better," she said, standing and running her hands down her body as if making sure all her curves and slender places were still where they ought to be.

"So?" I asked, grasping her hand. "Tell me the story. Where is Father Dear?"

"He's in the Third Valley where he belongs," she said. "Everything didn't go according to plan, but all is not lost. Not yet. I sent a man up to get you, but he found someone else outside and mixed you up. Why is everyone such a complete and utter idiot, Astrid?"

"I—I don't know," I said, trying to comprehend her words. She had sent a man to get me. "Was it the wolf prince?"

"No, just a shifter," she said, waving a dismissive hand. "The prince was injured, that's all I know. I'm going to visit them, but I needed a better body. I can hardly move around in that old lard-bag."

17

I glanced back at the strange, silent beauty of the old woman, feeling an odd urge to defend her.

"Anyhow, I'll be back, my dear," my mother said, taking my face in her hands and pinching both my cheeks at once. "Don't worry your silly little head. Wait for Mother Dear to take care of everything. You just stay here and look pretty, maybe add to your treasure."

Where else would I go? I'd never been out of this tower in my life. Until a few years ago, I'd never been out of this room. But for my thirteenth birthday, Father and Mother Dear had given me access to the trap door and the room below, where they kept my treasure so that no one would ever find it. Mother Dear always told me how much men liked treasure. It was my job to make sure they never got mine.

When she was gone, I stood at the window looking at the folds of land that formed the mountains and valleys below. I thought about painting, as I often sat there in summer and painted the view from my window, but I wasn't in the mood. Instead, I stared down at a path I could just make out through the trees. Mother Dear had said that she'd sent a man to get me.

Just a shifter. What shifter would she trust with her most precious treasure of all? She made it sound like it was just someone she'd passed on the trail, a random shifter she didn't even know. Shouldn't my father have come to get me? And what had happened to the prince I was to marry?

CAGED

I knew I should be worried about him. I should sit in my tower and pine for him and hope to be rescued like a maiden in a story. But I had no idea what the prince would be like, so it was hard to know what to worry about. So, I just sat in my tower and worried about my mother for the next two days. On the third day, I was sitting at my window waiting for a familiar figure on the path when a horse came tearing along into the field below my tower.

Stifling a shriek, I dropped down below the window, my heart hammering. After a minute, I slowly rose to peek over the sill. My eyes widened when I saw two people in the clearing. The horse had run away, and a naked man had appeared. My eyes widened. I had never seen a naked man, but his back looked wide and gloriously strong. I hadn't looked at my back in the mirror for a long time. I wondered if it looked that strong.

The people were fighting. Maybe the girl was mad that the man had chased her horse away. Pretty soon they pushed each other down and rolled around in the grass together. I gripped the sill, leaning forward, my heart pounding. The man was so big, he must be killing the girl! I wanted to scream, but I knew I wouldn't get there in time to save her. He held her down for a long time, until tears pooled in my eyes. I hadn't helped her. I hadn't even tried.

But then they got up, and they didn't even seem as angry anymore. My fingers had cramped around the sill, but I sagged in relief. She was okay. I didn't want to blink and miss a single moment. I hardly ever got to see people. When anyone came up onto the mountain from one of the valleys, I was supposed to go downstairs and hide. After all, they might try to find me and kill me.

But these people were busy focusing on each other…until they weren't. Suddenly, they were pointing and looking up at the tower—my tower. I fell backwards, scrambling on hands and feet away from the window, my heart flooding my chest until I thought I'd faint. After a minute, I convinced myself I'd been dreaming. Creeping back to the window, I listened hard. I could hear their voices, but not their words. I flattened myself against the wall and stepped toward the window, peeking out from one side this time. What I saw stopped my heart dead in my chest.

The man had shifted into a bird, and now he flew straight toward my window.

Chapter Four

Daniel

"Do you guys hear that?" I asked, cocking my head. Even though we were in human form, my sense of hearing was superior to all my herbivore brothers.

"What is it?" Jack asked. "I don't hear anything."

"It's a party," I said, a smile forming on my face. I liked to party.

"How do you know?" asked William, ever the pragmatist.

"I can hear it. Just through that gully, and down into the next valley."

Evan cocked an eyebrow at me.

"Weren't you listening to Ma?" William said.

"Yeah, but—"

"Bro, that's the witch valley," Jack said.

Evan just shook his head, looking disgusted.

"Your point is?" I asked, ignoring Evan and turning to Jack.

"We can't sell a cow to a witch," he said. "Not if the cow is going to turn back into William and disappear on them. They'll be pissed."

"And what if they won't let me go?" William said. "What if they trap me there and eat me?"

"Witches don't eat people," I said. "That's giants."

"And how did the witches get here?" Jack said.

Evan crossed his arms and planted his feet wide, frowning down at me.

"That's just a story," I said. "There's no other world full of giants and witches."

"Not a story," William said, pushing up his glasses. "We're living proof. Shapeshifting animals don't belong here, where everything makes logical human sense."

I appealed to Jack, the most adventurous of my brothers. "Come on, let's at least check it out. Whatever we descended from, we still need to eat."

"You're right," Jack said. "There's no reason we need to starve while the other two valleys are using diamonds as doorstoppers. Who cares what Ma said? She'll never know."

"Exactly," I said. "Her stories are as old as the ones about witches coming from other worlds. No witch has cursed anyone in our lifetime."

We turned to Evan for the final verdict. He scratched the back of his head and scrunched up his face, studying the gulley before us.

"Maybe there's a reason Ma told us not to go here," William said.

"Or maybe she doesn't understand witches, or maybe she just didn't want us to find more fun people to party with," I said. "Maybe they're not even witches at all. I mean, have you actually met a witch?"

"And I don't really want to walk all the way to town," Jack said.

Again, we turned to Evan, waiting for his wisdom. He shrugged and started forward, and the rest of us followed, our voices lowered in excitement.

"I've never been in the witch valley," Jack said. "This is going to be awesome."

"You think they really use diamonds as doorstoppers?" I asked.

"Shouldn't we be in animal form?" William asked.

"It's going to look weird to see a bunch of random animals running around in the woods together," Jack said. "Especially when one of them is a cow."

"Shut up," William said.

I slugged him in the shoulder. "Moooo."

He leaped at me, but Evan grabbed us both and held us apart, giving us a little shake to remind us that this was serious business, and if we were fighting and making a racket, they'd hear. We snuck down the rest of the mountain in silence. Just like I'd thought, there was a party going on. To be more precise, it looked like a wedding. Of course, I didn't know shit about witches, or weddings for that matter, but that's how it looked. Two people were standing at a stone altar holding hands while everyone else gathered around. For all I knew, they were about to do a human sacrifice.

And then the weirdest thing happened. A horse ran straight past us and down into the valley, right up to the wedding.

"Shit," Jack said. "Where did that thing come from?"

"Is that…?" William asked.

Before we could answer, the horse shifted into a man. Apparently, not all shifters were obeying the rule to stay out of the First Valley. I wasn't a bit surprised to see Efrain, one of the worse shifters in the valley, emerge from the horse form. There was a commotion among the witches, and I wished we'd gone charging in there instead of waiting up here. I couldn't even hear what they were saying with all of them talking at once. But we weren't as ballsy as Efrain. Most people weren't, though I knew Jack looked up to Efrain and his bad boy ways. He was a good eight or ten years older than us, and he was always fighting, or playing cards and drinking hard, or getting girls just to make them cry.

A few minutes later, the bride rode off on Efrain—in horse form—up the other side of the valley. The witches followed in a long procession.

"I don't know much about weddings, but I don't think that's supposed to happen," I said.

"But look," Jack said, pointing at two long picnic tables laden with packages wrapped in burlap, cardboard, pretty fabric, and paper. "We might not have to sell William today after all."

"Are we really going to steal from witches?" William asked.

"Do you want us to sell you to them instead?" Jack asked.

Even Evan shook his head in disbelief.

We waited until the witches had gone before emerging from behind the trees and running down the remaining hillside. The wedding had been taking place in a clearing surrounded by forest. The altar was at the far end, and on one side was a small, plain house with the gift tables set up in front of it.

"What is all this stuff?" William asked, picking up a box.

Evan ripped the wrapping off another package, which turned out to be a fancy stone pot.

"Man, this stuff is lame," Jack said.

Just then, the door to the little house opened. We all looked up, our mouths falling open as a man stepped out. He looked like giant. He was tall and broad, with dark brown skin and an eye patch that didn't quite cover all the scars on his cheek. Even in February, he was wearing a sleeveless T-shirt, and his arms were covered in scars, too. The guy looked like he'd eat all four of us for breakfast, whether we were in animal form or not.

Without a word, Evan shifted into a horse and took off. The rest of us followed, running toward the forest while stripping off our shirts. I prayed the giant wouldn't shoot me with a gun, or a spear, or a magical lightning bolt, or whatever witches had.

"Hey," he yelled after us, his voice a deep, resounding bark that followed me up the mountain. At the top, we stopped to regroup.

I shifted back into human form, though it was cold, and shrinkage was real. "What the hell was that?" I asked.

Evan shifted into his human form, too. William arrived in his bull form, huffing and puffing as he hobbled to a stop.

Jack, still in the form of a buck, scented the air.

"Nice rack," I said to him. He shifted back into human form then, as if he'd forgotten he was still an animal.

"Guess it's too late to sneak out without anyone seeing us," he said.

"Maybe it won't be too bad," I said. "We can tell them we came with Efrain."

"And face him?" William squeaked, still out of breath even though he'd shifted like the rest of us. "I'd rather face a witch."

"Hey, they didn't catch us," Jack said, spitting something into his palm.

"And it's not like we took anything," I said, looking around at the others.

Evan shook his head no, holding up his empty palms. Relief melted over me as I began to believe my own words. It would be okay.

"I might have taken something," Jack said.

"What?" I asked, rounding on him.

"It was in my hand," he protested. "It was just a tiny package. I thought it might be diamonds. Do you know how much we could sell those for? Ma would be set for life. We could get her a real house. And the witches would never miss them."

"Is it diamonds?" William asked, crowding closer to see what Jack had spit into his hand when he shifted back.

"No," he said, his shoulders slumping as he opened his palm. "It was a seed packet."

"So, you risked our lives for some pretty flowers," I said, disgusted.

"They're not flowers," Jack said. "They're beans."

Chapter Five

I stifled a scream and shrank away from the window. The man was coming. He was flying up here. Into my tower. Where no one had ever been before.

I dove for the bed, hitting the floor and sliding on my belly across the polished hardwood. I slid straight under the bed, inhaling a mouthful of dust. I really needed to sweep under here. I blinked cobwebs from my eyelashes as I heard the loud beat of wings. My heart hammered so hard I couldn't hear anything else for a minute. And then I heard a voice. Two voices, actually.

A deep voice like my father's, and a softer, plainer voice that belonged to a girl. They had flown up here. They must be shifters. Real shifters! Would I be their queen someday? Their hidden weapon?

I could hardly believe my ears. They were here, in the tower, with me. The girl was fawning over the woman in the bed above me. They sat right on top of the bed, right over me. I thought my heart would stop, but it kept right on beating as they discussed whether to leave or stay. The man left, and another man replaced him. And all the while, I laid there as quiet as a dead bug, just like Mother Dear had told me to do. Hide. I was good at hiding. I didn't even want to crawl out and meet them. Not even a little. I mean, what would I say?

Welcome to my tower. Would you like a tour? I've got a basket made of human hair, a shelf of books that I've basically memorized, and some clothes for when its cold. I'm not supposed to show you the room below this one, but it's full of treasure that need to be hidden so no one will steal it, just like me.

They sat on the bed again. I was getting really cramped. I was just starting to wonder if maybe I should slide out when the girl said, "Someone lives here."

And the man said, "Yeah."

My heart started racing a million miles a minute again. What if they were here to find me, and hurt me, and kill me? What if they took my treasure?

They sat and talked about traveling the world, seeing things. I had never thought of traveling the whole world. I just wanted to step on solid ground. This girl had a whole valley, and she wanted more. She was telling the man about how much she wanted it. Something strange happened to me then. It was like something inside me connected to something inside her, almost like when Mother Dear sent herself into another body. Except I was still in my body, and so was the girl. But her words slid into my heart like a knife. There was so much wanting in her, just like in me. She voiced the yearning in my own heart that I'd always been afraid to speak.

And instead of telling her she was stupid and ungrateful, that she was too weak to face a single valley let alone the whole world, the man told this girl that she could do it. My heart beat so loudly in my chest that I was sure they could hear. It was swelling inside me, cracking, growing bigger by the second, their words stuffing it with wonder and sadness and anger all at once. And then the girl stopped speaking, and I was sure she had felt the pull of my anguish as surely as I felt hers.

Her foot landed in a pile of my hair that I hadn't pulled under the bed, and I almost screamed with shock. She was going to lean down and look under, finding me at last.

Instead, she kicked my hair under. They weren't even looking for me. Reality snapped me back into my body. I wasn't connected to this girl. She was a stranger, and strangers were bad. Maybe they were trying to lure me out, waiting for me to show myself so they could pounce and trap me like an animal, the way they wanted to. They'd take me away and exploit my magic, strip away all I'd learned from my mother about chants and charms, and then they'd take my shifter crown and beat me until I cried so they could collect my tears. That's what Mother Dear said would happen if anyone found me.

Thank the stars, she came back into the body of the old woman before they found me. She could move between bodies much more easily when the bodies were right next to each other, but she was a talented sorceress and could do it even from far away. She took great pride in this fact. I wished I could do it, if only to walk around inside someone else for a day and see what the world looked like from ground level. But I knew that one day I would. I just had to be patient, and I'd live to see the whole world.

When Mother Dear lured them out the window, I closed my eyes and breathed a sigh of relief. A shudder wracked my body when I thought of how close I'd been to being discovered. Mother Dear was right. Next time, I would go through the trap door and disappear when someone came close to the tower. I stayed under the bed until the voices outside died away. I didn't know what had just happened. My brain could not make sense of the conversation that had taken place in this very room.

I went to my bookshelf and pulled out the World Atlas. I flipped through the pages, wondering what the girl wanted to see. The drawings were neat, and I had memorized nearly all the tiny words on every single one. Mother Dear had told me that they were places, and she'd even shown me the place where my lighthouse tower stood. I knew that the maps only represented places in the world. But I didn't really understand what the world was, how there could be so many places. The valleys I could see below looked infinite to me.

But not to other people. Today, I had been in the same room with some of these other people, people who had gone places and done things. Real, human people. Shifters who I would one day rule. It was almost like I'd talked to them. I mean, I could have, so it totally counted. They were practically my friends now. Everyone in the books I read had friends, and now I did, too. Sometimes, I saw people come into the clearing below and look for things, and I'd spend days making up stories about their lives. And this was even better!

So much better. It might last me for years. I could make up whole lives for these people, even pretend that they'd come to visit me. When I was quilting or painting or cooking, I could talk to them and pretend they were still sitting on the bed just behind me.

I had gotten so busy daydreaming about all the daydreaming I was going to do that I'd forgotten to move once they were gone. Now I scooted out from under the bed. My clothes were coated in dust. Oh, well. Now I had no need to sweep under there. I peeled off my dress and tossed it in my basket of dirty clothes. I didn't bother to get dressed again, though. Laundry took water, and a whole day of work, so I didn't do it often. Long ago, Mother Dear had enchanted the tower to stay at a comfortable temperature. Otherwise, I would have frozen as a baby, since the window didn't close.

I heard voices coming through it again, and my heart stutter-stepped in my chest. But I knew that in human form they couldn't fly up here, so I ran to the window to look. I hadn't seen so many people in my life. Just the random passerby in the field below. Today, I'd already seen the feet of the bird-man, the girl, and another man. Now I saw four more boys in the clearing below. They stood in a tight circle, gesturing and talking.

I leaned out a bit more, knowing they wouldn't look up. I knew because I studied every person that came into the clearing with complete devotion, memorizing their every move. Sometimes they dug around looking for things in the ground or in the trees, and some of them even circled my tower looking for a door that didn't exist. But no matter who they were or what they'd come for, they all did two things without fail.

When they came into the clearing, they let their heads drop back as they stared up at the tall tower where they couldn't go. After they'd looked at it, they never looked up again until they were ready to go. Then, sometimes they'd look up and sometimes not. But no one ever looked up while they were doing whatever they'd come for. That's when I could study them.

The four boys came close to the tower. One of them knelt just a few feet to the right of the window and dug his fingers into the dirt. He opened his palm and tilted it over the hole he'd made, covered the hole, and patted it with his palm.

From up high, I couldn't make out their faces, but I could see that two of them had hair like Mother Dear's, the beautiful color. Theirs was a bit darker, a gold color that shone in the sun. The other two had darker hair, a brilliant shade of brown that gleamed like a wet leaf in autumn.

Something rose up inside me, tingling along my spine and spreading through my limbs. I couldn't name the ache, the longing so deep within me that I hadn't known it was there. I wanted to talk to the boys. I wanted to call down to them and tell them I was here. That's all I wanted, it really was. It wasn't like I wanted them to sit on the edge of my bed and tell me all the places they wanted to go, like the girl had done earlier while I lay safely hidden away beneath her. It wasn't like I wanted that much. Just for someone to know that I existed, that I mattered.

But I knew I couldn't do that. I couldn't let them see me or they'd come up here like that bird-man. Still, I stood at the window, not stepping back to hide when they turned to go.

Look up, look up…

Maybe, if I didn't call to them but they saw me by themselves, Mother Dear wouldn't be too angry. I could say it had been an accident. It wasn't, though. I wasn't even hiding. I was standing in the window in plain view. For the first time in my life, I didn't just want to see someone outside a little closer, to know about them. I wanted them to know about me. As they walked away, I felt something inside me tightening, and I had to stifle the urge to cry out. I couldn't do that, though. That wasn't an accident.

Turn around, just one of you...

When they disappeared along the path, I sank to the floor in defeat. They probably couldn't see me from way down there, anyway. And if they did, they wouldn't want to come up and talk to me. What had I been thinking? They weren't boys I would roll in the grass and fight with. They were strangers, probably shifters, probably up to no good. What had they put in the ground, anyway? Would it break open a door in the side of the tower?

I should tell Mother Dear.

Instead, I went to the shelf and pulled out an encyclopedia. I looked at the faded grey pictures, trying to find any of the boys I'd seen below. I couldn't tell, so I pulled out a few of my story books and looked at the princes in the fairy tales. Maybe one of them was my future husband, a prince coming to rescue me. But it was no use. I hadn't seen their faces, so I couldn't match them to the boys in any of my books.

At last, I gave up and went about my daily tasks, singing as I cleaned and sewed, played music, and danced at an imaginary ball. Mother Dear said I had to know how to do all these things to charm my prince. She said I had the voice of a siren, and she would know, because she had once been one. When she was younger, she said, she could make anyone in the entire world fall in love with her with just a song. Mine wasn't as good as hers, though.

Mother Dear came the next day to tell me her plans had been foiled, but we weren't giving up yet. She was more determined than ever that I should be the shifter queen. I didn't know anything else, so life went on pretty much as usual for a few days. I was sitting on the windowsill singing and combing my hair as usual one day when I looked down and saw something bright green bursting up from the earth below my window.

My heart did a little flip. I ran to the shelf, pulled out my sketchbook, and rolled up a sheet of paper. Making a tube from it, I held it to my eye and examined the plant below. I couldn't tell much about it, but it had grown pretty big in the past week. It must be a few feet tall already. It wasn't in Mother Dear's way, so she wouldn't stomp it out like a weed.

"What are you thinking?" I asked myself aloud. "You should tell her. You should definitely tell her that some strange boys came and planted a rapidly growing vine that's climbing your wall."

I turned and paced back to the shelf, flattening the paper and placing it back in my sketch book. "But what if they're not coming to break a hole in the wall?" I asked. "What if they're the prince?"

When I was thoroughly confused, I decided to calm myself with painting another scene of the Ozark Mountains as seen from above. As always, I added peace eagles soaring in the sky. They could go anywhere, see anything. I sang as I worked and cleaned up. When I heard Mother Dear approaching, calling for the basket, I ran to the window. Below me...the vines had climbed at least a quarter of the way up the tower! Even though it was a warm spring day, and it had rained in the night, there was no way any plant could have grown ten feet in just a few hours. Not any normal plant, anyway.

Mother Dear wouldn't miss that. She would chop it down and demand to know who had planted it. And I should tell her. I should.

Instead, I whispered a quick disguising spell. It didn't make the vine invisible, exactly, just made it uninteresting. Mother Dear ignored it completely as she reached the bottom of the tower, even though it stretched far above her head on the wall just a few feet away. For a moment, I felt a smug satisfaction that I had done so well. I wasn't great at magic, despite being the daughter of a powerful sorceress. I was lucky if I could make a rock look like the shiny things Mother Dear collected downstairs. A more skilled witch could actually change a rock into one of them, though I didn't really understand why that was better.

All night, I waited for Mother Dear to mention the vines, but she didn't say a word. I should have said a word to her, should have told her that a vine was coming up to break into my room. But something had happened to me when that girl came to my room. She had wanted more than an entire valley, and now I wanted something I'd never wanted before, too. I'd always looked forward to the day I could leave my tower, but now I wanted more. I wanted to see the world—not the whole world, like she'd wanted, but the real world, where other people lived and laughed and planted seeds and wrestled in the grass. And I wanted the world to see me.

Every day after that, I reached as far as I could out the window and dumped a bit of water on the vines and sang to them. Maybe I couldn't make a boy fall in love with me with my song, but I was sure I was making the plant grow. Every day, they grew higher, until they were a wild tangle that threatened to encroach on my basket's path. Mother Dear wouldn't be able to ignore them then. The thought made my heart race with panic. What would I do then?

One warm morning I asked Mother Dear for water to do laundry. As I sat on my heels sloshing them in the tub, I sang to pass the time. Gathering an armload of sodden clothes, I headed to the window to hang them out to dry. I set the pile on the windowsill and leaned out, shaking the wrinkles from a skirt.

"Hello up there," a voice called.

I screamed, flinging the skirt high into the air. It sailed down like a soggy shroud and wrapped around the boy perched in the vines reaching halfway to my window.

Chapter Six

William

By the time I struggled free of the clinging wet sheet the girl had hurled at me, she was gone. I hadn't even known she was there. It was my turn to water the plant, so I'd come up to the mountain. The moment I'd heard her voice, I knew I had to see her. The voice was the purest, most beautiful sound I'd ever heard, a voice straight from the mouth of an angel. There was no other explanation. So, I had started climbing the vine. Maybe it led to heaven. It was obviously not of this world, so why not?

I tossed the soggy sheet aside and climbed the rest of the way up the vine, until it started pulling free of the wall. That's when some sense came back into my head, and I realized I was fifty feet above a layer of unforgiving rocky Ozark soil. I really hoped this wasn't some kind of poison ivy on steroids, because I was butt-ass naked after shifting into human form.

"Hey," I yelled. "I won't hurt you. I heard you singing, that's all."

For a minute, no sound came from the tower, and I thought she wouldn't answer. But then a little voice drifted down. "Really?"

"Yeah, really," I said. "You scared me. I didn't know anyone was up there."

A head of coppery hair appeared slowly over the windowsill, the face appearing inch by inch, stopping when her huge eyes were exposed. "I scared you?"

"I mean, you startled me," I said. "I'm not afraid of a girl. You just surprised me. How'd you get in there?"

"I—I'm not supposed to tell."

I couldn't help but laugh at that. "Why not?"

"Because you're a stranger," she said. "I'm not supposed to talk to strangers."

"Too late," I said, offering her a grin. "You're already talking to me."

She clapped a hand over her mouth, rising up a little more so I could see her whole face. She was pretty, but there was something else about her, something that went beyond pretty. She looked delicate and new somehow, like a newborn fawn.

"I'm William," I said. "Who are you?"

"I'm not supposed to tell you that, either."

"Okay," I said. "How about a name? Can you tell me that? A name doesn't really tell me who you are. It doesn't really tell me anything, does it?"

She squinted, her eyes suspicious. "How do I know you won't hurt me?"

"With what?" I asked. "If I let go of this vine, I'll fall. I have no weapons. In case you can't see past all these leaves, I'm actually not wearing anything."

I was pretty glad for the leafy coverage. I'd climbed the mountain in animal form, and I hadn't expected to run into anyone, so I hadn't stashed clothes anywhere. Now that I knew someone lived here, I'd be bringing clothes for my next visit.

"Me, neither," the girl said. "I was washing my clothes, not wearing them."

Now I was really, really glad for the leafy coverage. I would have thought she was teasing me, but she nothing in her face hinted at a joke. Any other naked girl would have thrown her wash water on my head if I told her I was also naked. Unless she was a shifter. Shifters usually weren't super modest, since we spent a lot of time shifting and finding ourselves without clothes around. I figured it was a pretty safe guess, so I went ahead and asked.

"You're a shifter?"

As soon as I said it, I regretted it. Her face changed, the innocent openness slamming shut and a guarded expression taking over.

"Sorry," I said. "Uh, don't tell me. You don't have to tell me anything. But since you know my name, we're not strangers anymore, so we can talk. Right?"

I couldn't think of another explanation for her nakedness, but I knew I wasn't done talking to her. Something about her fascinated me, though I didn't know why. To be real, it was probably just the nakedness.

"What's that plant?" she asked, nodding at the vines I clung to.

"I don't know," I admitted. "We kinda stole it from the witches at the wedding."

"Witches?" Her eyes widened. "Wedding? Who got married?"

"Some redheaded witch," I said, trying to study her without staring and totally freaking her out.

"Are you married?"

A snort-laugh escaped me at the thought. "No," I said. "Are you?"

"No," she said. "Mother Dear doesn't want me talking to anyone, so I can't get married unless I meet the prince."

"Right," I said, adjusting my weight on the vine. "Want to come down so we can talk without having to yell at each other?"

"Oh, I can't."

We stared at each other for a good ten seconds. "You're stuck up there?"

"I'm not allowed to leave," she said, like that was different from what I'd said.

"Why not?"

"Because someone might steal me," she said. "Mother Dear says it's the only place that's safe."

I was starting to get a really weird feeling about this mother of hers. "When was the last time you left?"

"When I was a baby," she said. "I wasn't born here."

"Wait, you've never left? Ever?"

"There's no door," she said. "That's so no one can get in and get me. But it also means I can't get out. It's unfortunate, but that's the way it has to be."

"You're not a shifter?"

"Mother Dear says I'm not supposed to tell anyone anything about me," she said, looking truly regretful. "She went to get more water for washing, but she's on her way back, so…"

"I should go," I finished for her. I had no desire to meet this crazy mother of hers, but I wanted to stay. I wanted to figure out who she was, and why she was there, and what the hell she was doing up there. I couldn't wait to go home and tell my brothers about this. There wasn't just a lighthouse with no doors on top of the mountain. It had a crazy girl living in it.

"I'll ask Mother Dear if I can come down next time," she said. "Since you're not a stranger now."

"I don't know if I should come back," I said. "I mean, I didn't get your name. So, you're a stranger to me."

Her eyes widened. "Oh," she said. "That's true. In that case, I'm Astrid."

"Hi, Astrid," I said, trying out her name. "Nice to meet you."

Nice wasn't quite the word I was thinking. More like surreal and bat-shit crazy.

"Hi," she said, beaming at me. "I'm so happy you came to visit. I've never had a visitor."

"You've lived up there all your life without ever seeing anyone?"

"Oh, no," she said. "I see Mother Dear. And a couple times, Father Dear came to see me."

"Jesus," I muttered. "Okay, Astrid. Well, I'll come back, okay? If you want me to."

She nodded vigorously. Suddenly, her gaze flickered to the woods behind me, and her eyes widened even further. "Hide," she said, her voice nothing but a gasp.

"What?"

"Mother Dear is coming," she said. "Hide in the leaves. Otherwise she'll kill you."

The urgency in her voice said she wasn't kidding around. Shifters were pretty rough, but people didn't just kill each other. But the way she said it, well, I wasn't going to wait around and see which one was crazier, the girl or her dear mother.

"Astrid," a high voice called from a little way off.

Cursing quietly, I started down, lowering myself hand over hand.

"Hide," Astrid hissed. "You don't have time." She was right. Even if I reached the bottom, I'd have to run into the woods to hide. The trees were starting to leaf out, but they weren't thick enough to hide me yet, and there weren't any good boulders close by. I wondered what her mother thought of this miraculous bean plant, but I wasn't about to ask. Instead, I followed Astrid's orders and burrowed into the leafy vines.

"Why didn't you answer me, silly girl," said her mother's voice, closer than I liked.

"Sorry, sorry," Astrid said from above.

"We've got to do something about these vines," her mother said.

"Oh!" Astrid said as something large and brownish red fell past me. "Sorry, Mother Dear. I didn't mean to drop that on you."

At first, I thought she'd dropped more of her wet laundry to distract her mother. It worked, but it wasn't laundry. Her mother picked up the huge, flexible basket and set a bucket of water into it. I looked up to see Astrid leaning out her window, arranging the rope attached to the handle. When she leaned back inside, the basket began to rise.

And I'd thought we had it bad going to a laundromat.

After a couple minutes, the basket lowered again, and the woman climbed into it. I flattened my back against the tower wall, praying to Odin, Zeus, Ra, and all the other gods I could think of that she wouldn't turn and look straight into my face. There was a gap in the leaves I'd been using to see everything, but that meant she could probably see me. As she rose past my hiding place, a splash of recognition hit me like she'd dumped the bucket of icy spring water on my head.

I knew the woman. Well, I didn't know her. But I knew who she was—everyone did. She was the only witch who came into the shifter valley. She and the deadbeat shifter king had a thing going on. Which meant that Astrid wasn't a shifter. She was a witch.

A chill shivered down my spine.

"I brought some things for dinner," her mother said.

"Can you stay?" Astrid asked, her voice full of a heartbreaking amount of hope. The girl really didn't see anyone else. I tried to comprehend that, to wrap my head around how absolutely lonely it must be. I had three brothers around me, and though they could be pains in the asses more often than not, I couldn't imagine not having them.

Sure, they teased me about being a cow, always having my nose buried in a book of legends, and striking out with every girl in the Second Valley. But if I needed them, they had my back. When I got picked on at school for being scrawny, they told the bully that the four of us together were still three times as big as him. When my one girlfriend in high school broke my heart, Jack said he'd try to make her fall in love with him so he could break her heart in return. Hell, when Dad took off and Mom worked nights, they'd fed me bottles and changed my diapers. We ate together, drank together, got in trouble together. If I had to live in a lighthouse all by myself, I'd have gone totally bonkers, too.

When I heard them talking above, I dared to slide a foot down the vines a bit. The leaves shook, and I froze, squeezing my eyes shut.

"Did you hear something?" asked the mother witch, Yvonne.

"Just the wind," Astrid said.

"It's that damn vine," Yvonne said. "I'd better cut that down. I didn't think it would grow so tall."

"Let's make dinner first," Astrid said. "What did you bring?"

I breathed a sigh of relief and made my way one agonizing, slow step at a time. Astrid might be a witch, but she was definitely protecting me. I just didn't know why.

Chapter Seven

Astrid

I loved cooking with Mother Dear. Usually she left me food and had to rush off to see Father, or work in the First Valley, or whatever else she did. My bed was big enough for both of us, but more often than not, I slept beside an empty body. They weren't dead, just sleeping deeply. They still breathed, so it was almost like having a real person there. That's why I talked to them. Still, it was nice to have Mother Dear there to answer when I talked to her.

"Mother Dear," I started. "Where do the bodies come from?"

"What?" she asked, pausing with the chopping knife poised above a beet.

"The bodies you use as disguises," I said. "Where do you get them?"

"Oh, different places," she said with a tinkling laugh. "Sometimes, like the last old lady, she had died. I gave her life for a few more days."

"That's nice of you," I said, tossing some onions into the pot. It wasn't exactly like Mother Dear had given her extra life, though, was it? She had slept here, or she'd been taken out as a disguise. She hadn't actually experienced those extra days—Mother Dear had experienced them while inside her body. It was kind of like what I did. I got to be here, breathing and reading and eating, but I didn't actually get to experience anything new. It was the same thing day after day for sixteen years.

"Do you think I could do that?" I asked.

"Do what, dear?" she asked, slicing into a thick red slab of beet flesh.

"What you do?" I said. "Think about it. I know I can't leave here because someone might see me and take me. But if I was in someone else's body, no one would recognize me, so I'd be safe."

Mother Dear scooped the chopped beets into her hands and dropped them into the pot. My eyes fell on the silver blade, now smeared with red juices.

"I'm surprised at you," she said. "After all I've done to make this place perfect for you, this is the thanks I get? You have untold riches at your disposal, Astrid. You're probably the richest girl in the world. You use drops of gold as your playthings, and you want to walk away from it all to mingle with the commoners? They're dirty, half-starved, depraved hoodlums, Astrid. They'd take one look at you and set upon you like vultures."

"But if I was in a disguise—"

"Why are you doing this?" Mother asked, whirling on me. Her eyes flashed, then narrowed, and I was sure she could see the deception on me like a stain. She'd told me about the liars and thieves down there in the valleys, in the rest of the world. Here, things were good and pure and honest. Here, I never lied.

But I had. I had deceived her with a spell on the vines, and now with the boy who had climbed them. Maybe I wasn't fit to be the princess after all. Maybe, deep down inside, I was just like everyone else in the world out there. Maybe Mother Dear had the wrong person. I didn't feel like a princess. I just felt scared.

"I just wondered," I said. "It's okay, Mother Dear. I don't have to go out. I just wanted to know what it was like out there. Really know."

"It's awful, that's what it's like," she said, her fingers clenching around the handle of the knife. "And why you would think of betraying me after all I've done for you…I can't imagine. Did I teach you to be this selfish and ungrateful?"

"No," I said quickly. "I'm sorry. I didn't mean to be."

"Haven't I fed you every day of your life, brought you clean water and given you the safest home in all the world? I sacrificed my own place in your father's life, so I could stay close to you even when he moved away. I've saved nearly every tear you've ever cried, going without while you wallow in riches, all so that you'll have something to bring the shifters when you become their queen. Do you think the coven would simply look the other way if they knew what you can do? No, they would take your treasure and take you with it, milking tears from you like a cash cow."

"Yes, Mother Dear," I said. I knew not to argue once she got going.

"Once people found out, they would never let you stop crying. They won't see you as a beautiful princess, as I do. They will see you as someone who can give you all they've ever dreamed of. That's how the world will see you, Astrid. That's why I must keep you a secret."

"Yes, Mother Dear."

"No one will love you if they know," she said. "They'll only use you. Even when you are married, you must only give your husband a bit, and never tell him where they come from. There is no end to human greed, and even if he loves you at first, once he knows what you can do for him, he will see you differently. He will see you as less than human, and you will become a slave to your own tears."

"I know," I whispered.

"What would I do without my precious daughter?" Her voice softened, and she set down the knife and took my hands in hers. "I would die without you, my dear. You're my whole life." She pulled me in and pressed my head to her chest, stroking my hair.

Tears of shame burned at the back of my eyes. Mother Dear had given up her life for me, and she'd given me a wonderful life, and I knew that she would die if she lost me. She told me so all the time. If I kept a secret, she might die, too.

"I have to tell you something," I said, choking back a sob and clinging to her. "There was a boy here. He was climbing the vine, and he saw me. I talked to him."

Mother's shoulders went stiff, and her hand stilled. "What boy?"

"He was a shifter," I said. "His name is William." The terrible, smothering weight of my deception lifted as I spoke, and I could breathe right for the first time in weeks, when I'd first seen them planting the seeds.

"Is that right?" she asked through clenched teeth. Her voice remained sweet, though, so I wasn't afraid.

"I won't do it again," I said. "I promise. I'll hide like you said, even if he sees me."

"Yes, you will," she said. "I'll get rid of the vine, so he can't come back."

"No," I gasped, gripping her shoulders. "It's… I like the vine."

"I know, dear," she said. "But would you also like to die?"

I pulled back, my eyes wide as I shook my head. "No, Mother Dear. But he wasn't going to hurt me. He said so."

"Oh, my beautiful, dumb daughter," she said, stroking my hair behind my ear. "Boys will say anything to get what they want. They'll tell you one thing, but they actually mean the opposite. When he says he's not here to hurt you, what he means is that he's actually here to do much worse. He's here to steal your treasure and keep you from taking your rightful place as queen."

I nodded, wiping away a tear. If I wiped them before they fell, they never turned to gold. "Okay."

"If you want to live, you'll have to scare him away. Now that he knows you live here, he'll be back. A young body like yours is a siren song in itself, especially to greedy men like him. I'll cut down the vines, and you must dump boiling water on him if he comes back."

I nodded again. "Okay, I'll do that. But can you just... leave the vines? I like them. They're like friends to me. I talk to them. They like my songs."

"Don't worry, my dear," she said. "I'm working hard to get you out of here. You must be patient and wait until the time is right, when it's safe. You'll have more friends than you know what to do with when you're queen."

"But I thought you said I couldn't trust anyone down there."

"That's why I'll be there," she said. "I know how to tell who can be trusted, and I'll be with you every step of the way. I'll never leave your side, Astrid."

"Promise?" I asked, thinking of the boy with luminous bronze hair and kind eyes behind his glasses. He had looked so sincere.

"I promise," Mother Dear said. "Now, wipe your face. You're not a pretty crier, Astrid. You should avoid that. A princess must always appear young and beautiful and poised."

I nodded, turning away to go wash my face in the basin and dress like a princess, in one of the fine dresses Mother Dear had given me. Most of them were scratchy or heavy or hot, but it didn't matter. From now on, I would be good and wait for my time, like Mother Dear wanted.

Still, I hid in the bed and cried when she cut down the vines.

Chapter Eight

Astrid

Days went by, and everything returned to normal. At least everything appeared normal. Inside me, a hole had opened, and nothing could fill it. I ate, and danced, and sang, and painted, and counted gold in the room full of treasure that was supposed to be mine. But nothing worked. I had grown dull. I would have traded the shiniest gold in the world for one afternoon with a human who talked to me.

One day as I sat piecing a quilt, I heard an exclamation outside. I lifted my head from my work, listening. It was a boy's voice, and my heart leapt in my chest before sinking back to my toes. I stared at the stitches I'd made, but my fingers refused to move.

"Astrid," he called. "Are you up there?"

I swallowed hard and pinched my lips together, almost choking on the knot of longing lodged in my throat, rendering me silent. If I talked to him, Mother Dear might do something drastic.

"If you're up there, sing something," he called. He sounded too close, closer than the ground. My heart leapt up and took off racing at the sound. He'd told me he was a shifter, but he hadn't told me what kind. Maybe he was a bird like the man in the field, and he'd come up to see me. I'd told Mother Dear I wouldn't talk to him, but I hadn't said I wouldn't look. To prove that I was following her orders, I put a pan of water on the stove. Then I crept to the window on trembling legs.

It wasn't William. It was one of the other boys, one with golden hair and blue eyes. "My brother has been raving about your voice for a week," he said. "I swear, the guy's obsessed. He can't go five minutes without talking about you. Just sing me a note so I know you're alive in there."

I had promised I wouldn't speak, but I hadn't said anything about singing.

But what if he was there to steal my treasure? Or my life?

"Okay, I knew it," he said. "There's no singing girl in the tower, and I'm out here talking to myself like a dumbass. Not to mention I'm fifty feet from the ground on a dead vine. I'm going to kill William."

"No," I cried, leaping over to the window.

The boy let out a yelp of surprise and jerked back, and the dead vine cracked. It began to slide slowly sideways. He grappled at the wall, terror taking over his expression.

"No," I cried again, my hand shooting out, though it was nowhere near him. Without thinking I grabbed my braid and tossed it down to him. His fingers closed around it, and his eyes locked on mine, full of blind panic.

"Stay calm," I said, gripping the sill with both hands and trying not to cry out in pain. I was afraid he was going to yank me right out the window. "You're not sliding anymore. You're not falling. Just calm down. Tell me your name."

"I'm stuck," he said. "The vine won't hold me. I can't fall fifty feet. I'll die."

"It's more than that," I squeaked. It was true. The vine seemed to have died, but somehow, had continued to climb. It was almost to my window. Maybe only ten feet below.

The boy closed his eyes and whispered, "Fuck. William's gone too far with the pranking."

"But I'm really here," I said. "He didn't trick you, right? I'm here, and I'll help you. Just…just climb up my hair."

His eyes snapped open, and he looked at me like I was crazy. "I can't. I'll pull you out. Then we'll both die."

"Okay, just hold on a second," I said. "I'll see if I can reach the basket."

"What basket?" At least he looked sane and rational now. I didn't have time to answer his questions though. My scalp felt like it was ripping from my head. I scooted sideways, reaching blindly for the basket. My fingers brushed the prickly hair, but I couldn't lift it off the hook from my position at the sill. I couldn't straighten at all with his weight hanging on my head.

I squeezed my eyes closed, trying to summon some magic. A chant that would lift the basket, though I had no elemental magic. I was like Mother Dear, who couldn't turn stone to gold or lift a basket with an artificial wind.

I heard a cracking sound below, and the weight on my head jerked harder. We both cried out, and I almost pitched out the window. I was bent double over the sill, gripping it with both hands.

"I'm letting go," the boy said. "I'm Jack, by the way. If you need to…notify my family."

"Don't you dare," I hissed. "Now shut up and let me get the basket."

I found a summoning chant somewhere in the recesses of my mind. Bracing my feet wide, I wedged my knees against the wall and reached up with one hand again, calling to the basket with my mind as I whispered a chant. I thought my entire scalp would come loose before it dropped into my hand. With a sob of relief, I threw it out the window to Jack.

A second later, the weight lifted from my head, and the rope holding the basket began to unspool. I grabbed it and held on, bracing my feet the way I did when I hauled Mother Dear up. Hand over hand, I drew it up until Jack was even with the window. He grabbed the sill and hopped nimbly from the basket and landed on the floor beside me.

"Thanks," he said with a grin.

All words deserted me. I'd never seen anyone but my parents like this, and Jack wasn't like my parents. He was so...different. His hair was curly and golden, and his skin was smooth and tan like he'd spent a lot of time outdoors. But it was more than that. An energy radiated from him, frenetic and bright as the sun. I'd seen his face, and his brother's, but they'd been far below. Now he was on level ground, staring straight at me. I had the sudden urge to run behind the bed and hide.

He gaped at me, his mouth dropping open. His eyes got so round I could see the white all around the blue irises. A funny little lump on the front of his throat moved up and down.

"Why are you naked?" he asked, his voice sounding funny, too. I wondered if he had something stuck in his throat.

"Because it's warm today," I said. "Why are you dressed?"

"I...I don't know," he said, his smile returning. His eyes were squinty at the corners when he smiled, like they were in on the joke along with his mouth. "That's a great question. Would it make you more comfortable if I was naked, too?"

"It would probably make you more comfortable," I said. "I'm comfortable already."

He grinned, biting down on his bottom lip. I found my eyes riveted to the edge of his white teeth cutting into his pink lip. Hooking his thumbs in the band of his navy-blue sweatpants, he paused, his eyes still on my face. He was watching me like he expected something, but I didn't know what.

"You sure about this?" he asked, cocking his head to one side.

I nodded, a strange mixture of anticipation and nervousness racing along my synapses. He was acting so strange. I knew that princesses didn't go around like this, without clothes, but he didn't know I was a princess, so it didn't matter what I looked like to him. But maybe he was a prince, and that's why he was being strange about it.

Before I could ask, he grabbed the bottom of his grey T-shirt and peeled it off over his head. I drew a breath. His skin was tanned and seemed to radiate with the same energy as the rest of him, as if I could see the heat rising from it. My fingers twitched, longing to reach out and touch him.

"Have you ever seen a guy naked before?" Jack asked.

I shook my head. My heart had started to pound, a cloudiness seeming to hover above my brain. My skin felt hot even though I didn't have extra clothes on.

"Did my awesome abs render you speechless?" Jack asked, flexing his arms. His muscles bulged, and the ones in his abdomen rippled in little ridges that drew my eyes down them. His sweatpants hung low on his hips, so low I could see his hipbones and the small muscles that led along the inner rim of them. I swallowed, my heart skipping a beat.

CAGED

"Apparently so," he muttered, dropping his arms. He was looking at me a little strangely now, the smile gone from his face.

"I saw your brother naked the other day," I said when I realized he was waiting for a response.

"Did you?" Jack said, the smile returning.

I relaxed a little and nodded hard.

"He didn't tell me that part," Jack said. "So…uh…what'd you think?"

"About what?"

He laughed and picked up his shirt from the floor. "Believe me, I'd love to get naked with you, but I don't think you're ready for all this."

"All what?" I asked.

"All five feet ten inches of Jack Jameson," he said, holding out his shirt to me. "And if anyone asks, this never happened. I'd lose serious man points for refusing to get naked with a girl who looks like you."

I took his shirt. It was thin and worn, and I held it to my cheek to feel its feather softness. It smelled like nothing I'd ever smelled before—like sweat, and the woods outside, and something warm and animal and salty that I'd never encountered. Burying my nose in it, I inhaled deeply. The scent was dizzying, intoxicating. It did something strange to my body, as if it had transferred some of the buzzing energy radiating from him into me. I breathed in again, so deep it made me almost lightheaded.

That's when I noticed Jack staring at me with wide-eyed awe. "Who are you?" he whispered.

Oh no. Maybe I'd given myself away. Maybe he knew I was the princess, and I wasn't acting at all like one. I should be wearing one of the fine dresses.

"I'm Astrid," I said.

"You really do live here," he said. "I thought my brother was making that up. You've really never left this place, have you?"

I shook my head.

Jack pressed his lips together for a long moment. Then he said, "Put on the shirt."

I obeyed, though once I'd pulled it over my head, I had to drag my braid up through the neck. The shirt started to rise, but Jack stepped forward and grabbed the hem, holding it down over my hips while I pulled my braid up loop after loop until it was free of the shirt. That's when I realized how close we were standing. I could feel the heat of his body, not just see it. His bare chest was so close, and even though it was warm, and the day was warm, and I was wearing a shirt, I felt my nipples pinch like it was winter outside.

Some strange force caught my eyes and made them meet his. It was like they were trapped by his gaze. I swallowed hard. Jack's knuckles grazed my thigh, and my whole body trembled. I grabbed his upper arms to steady myself, and another shock went through me. His body was so hot, so solid. Alive and real like an animal. His skin was soft over hard muscle just like mine, though. Not like an animal. Like a person.

"Are you a shifter?" I asked.

He nodded. "A buck. You?"

"A turtle."

The corner of his mouth quirked up. "You're no turtle, Astrid."

"What?" I whispered, my heart stammering in my chest. I couldn't think right with him here. I couldn't breathe right. Everything inside my body was shimmering, and turning cartwheels, and flying against the walls of my body like a thousand caged birds.

"You're a fox," Jack said.

I thought about how hard I had tried to turn into a turtle all those times. I had done it. I had seen my turtle feet, had struggled on my turtle shell when Mother Dear set me on my back so I could see how dangerous it would be to shift without her there. I could fall and get stuck on my back and then what would happen to me?

When I shook my head, Jack chuckled and released his hold on my shirt. I held onto his arms, letting him drag me a step forward when he stepped back. I couldn't bear the thought of letting him go yet. His skin was so warm, so golden. He had nipples like mine but flatter and browner, and ridges of muscle I didn't have. His chest looked hard instead of soft, and he had little hairs around his belly button that looked as soft as the ones at the nape of my neck.

"Can I touch you?" I asked, unable to resist the call of his bare skin.

That funny little bump in his throat moved up and down. "What?"

"I've never seen a real boy before," I said. "You look different than me. Do you feel different?"

"I'm not actually sure how I feel right now," Jack said. "This has been by far the weirdest day of my entire life. I'm still waiting for my brothers to step out from behind the curtain and laugh their asses off at me."

He didn't move away, so I released one of his arms and pressed my fingertips to his chest. It was hard, like it looked. Not like mine at all. I moved my fingers up, pressing higher, then moving around his nipple. It pinched up just like mine.

"This is so weird," Jack said, letting out a funny little laugh that was half breath and half voice.

I flattened my hand over his heart, feeling the steady, rapid beat of his life's rhythm inside him. My own heartbeat picked up speed as if trying to catch up to his, and that wobbly feeling returned to my legs. I slid my hand lower, skimming over the ridges of muscle in his stomach. His skin prickled under my fingertips despite warmth in the room.

"Astrid." His voice sounded different, like that thing stuck in his throat was bothering him.

"Yes?" I asked, too enthralled by his body to look away. I slid my hands down his sides, palming his hipbones.

He cleared his throat. "I'm feeling a little exposed here. Not that I don't like what you're doing. Obviously. I'm just wearing sweatpants, and it's getting awkward, you know? Maybe I could sit down for a minute and, uh, cool off?"

I slid my hands around him, up his back. His shoulder blades were bigger than my entire hands. Jack's eyes widened as our bodies came into contact.

"Way to make things less awkward," he muttered.

"Why are things awkward?" I asked. His eyes were so close I could see the flecks of darker blue in his sky-colored irises. His lips were full and smooth, no longer smiling.

"Because you're touching me, and I wouldn't feel right touching you."

"Why?" I asked. "Have you ever seen a girl before?"

He made a little choked sound. "Yeah, but... Not one like you."

"You can touch me," I offered. "Want me to take my shirt off again?"

"No," he said quickly. "I mean, I do. I would. You're hot and everything, but you're like a kid or something. It's not right."

"It's okay," I said, lifting his hand and setting it on my hip. "Go on. You can touch me, too."

He closed his eyes, his hand moving to my waist and his face dropping next to mine. "Oh, wow," he whispered, tugging me closer, so our bodies were pressed together. I could feel his heart beating against mine through the thin shirt. He inhaled deeply, nuzzling against my neck. My hands moved down his back again, marveling at the muscles I didn't know existed on my own body. My face fit into the arch of his neck, and the smell of him filled me from my nose all the way down to my toes. Suddenly, my knees weren't the only part of me doing something strange. A warm pressure built between my thighs, and I pulled Jack against me as if he could fix it.

His hands tightened on my waist, but then he stepped back, breaking our embrace. And even though I'd hugged my mother before, and even my father, it had never been like that. Those hugs had never left me breathless and wanting for something I couldn't name. They hadn't filled my body with stars like the summer sky at night, hadn't shimmered through my blood like the sun on icicles in winter.

"I'm sorry," he said. "I can't. This is too fucking weird, Astrid. Call me a pussy or take my man card or whatever, but this is really freaking me out."

"Sorry, sorry," I said, not really knowing what just happened. I was too confused to process it, but I knew by his tone that he wasn't happy. I had a lot of experience disappointing people, and I seemed to have done it without trying, as usual.

"You're not the one who should be sorry," Jack said, reaching out and lifting my braid, holding it up and scanning the length. "How's your head, anyway?"

"Fine," I said. I'd forgotten about the hurt, but I knew I'd be feeling it for days. "And that's not your fault. You didn't try to fall."

"That's not what I meant," Jack said, dropping my braid. "I meant your mother. Have you ever even had a haircut? Or, I don't know, learned to read? Tied your shoes?"

"I know how to read," I said, drawing back indignantly. "I've read at least ten encyclopedias. I'd read more, but that's all I have. And my hair just grows really fast. I've cut it before. That's what I used to make the basket that saved your life."

"Jesus," he muttered, rubbing a hand over his messy golden curls. "Every time I think this can't get any weirder, it does."

"You're the one who climbed up and wanted to see me," I said, crossing my arms over my chest.

"You're right," he said. "And now that I have, I've got to get you out of here."

"Out?" I asked, my heart stammering at the thought. "Why?"

"Because you're like... I don't even know the word. Abused? Neglected? Freakishly sheltered?"

"I'm not abused," I said. "Mother Dear loves me. And I can't just leave. It would kill her."

"I think staying might kill you."

"I've been here sixteen years, and I'm fine," I said.

"And you don't want to leave? You've never wanted to walk on solid ground, feel the dirt between your toes, or look up at a tree, or talk to someone besides your mother?"

My heart squeezed so tight at his words that I almost couldn't speak. "I have."

"I'll take you to my house," he said. "We don't have much, or anything, really. But you'd have us."

"I'm not allowed to leave."

"Don't you ever disobey your mother?"

"No," I said with a huff. "Why would I do that?"

"Because that's what sixteen-year-old girls do," he said, flashing me a grin that lit me up like dawn over the mountains. "Now, let's get out of here."

"Mother Dear will come back and see that I'm gone," I said, tugging at the hem of his shirt, which hit just below the point where my thighs met. "She'll come find me. I can't leave."

Jack rounded on me, fisting his hands on his hips. "Why not? Give me a better reason."

"Because," I said, my voice starting to shake. "If I did, someone might take me away. They'd lock me up, so I could never be free, and they'd steal my magic and my treasure. Mother Dear told me. I can't leave until the wolf prince wants to marry me."

Jack stared at me, his eyes getting bigger and bigger. "You're not allowed to leave," he said. "Ever."

I shook my head.

His eyes went soft, and his voice did, too. "You're a prisoner already, Astrid."

"No," I said, shaking my head harder as I backed away from him. But the truth of his words sank into me like heavy stones. My legs started trembling, this time for an entirely different reason. I didn't want to believe it. I wanted to be here, to be loved by my mother, to have everything I needed, just like she always told me I did.

Jack crossed his arms and rocked back on his heels. "She'd hunt you down and bring you back if you tried to leave."

"But when I'm here, I'm free." I sank onto the edge of the bed. I repeated the word, speaking to myself, as if that could make it true. "I'm free."

"Yeah," he said. "Free in your cage."

Chapter Nine

Evan

"I told you I wasn't making shit up," William said, pushing up his glasses. We'd built a bonfire in the backyard and sat around it on milk crates listening to Jack's crazy story.

"Now you're both bullshitting us," Daniel said. "I mean, you're the bull after all. Bullshit is your specialty."

William took a swipe at him, which I interrupted. I handed everyone a can of beer, so we could settle down and figure out what to do.

"We've got to get her out of there," Jack said. "I'm telling you, it was insane. You won't even believe it when you see it. She lives in this crazy make-believe world her mother built for her."

I raised an eyebrow and tilted my head toward the house.

Jack faltered, his animated expression dimming. His shoulders slumped, and he stared down at his unopened beer.

"You're right," he said. "We can't bring her here. It's probably worse than where she is now."

We sat sipping our beers in silence.

"I want to go see her," Daniel said at last, stretching his legs toward the bonfire. I nodded in agreement. There had to be something we could do. We couldn't bring her here, though. We didn't have enough money to feed ourselves most of the time. I'd gotten a job working on an apple orchard in the valley that would pay me under the table, but half the time, the guy paid in beer. Not to mention we didn't have an extra bed. The four of us still had to share a bedroom, and we were way too old for that.

I thought about tracking down our old man, but he didn't have any money to spare. Not that he'd even acknowledge us. He had a new family now, some other shifter woman who'd put up with his shit for longer than our mothers had. Sometimes I saw him around the valley, filling up at the lone gas station or driving by in his sad old pickup truck. Unlike a couple of my brothers, I didn't blame the guy. No one in our valley had money. He worked like everyone else and gave what little he could to the woman who had stayed with him. Her kids might eat a little better than we did, but I couldn't begrudge them that. None of us had asked to come into the world, let alone the shifter world.

"We've got to do something," William said. "We can't just leave her."

"We also can't kidnap her," Jack said.

I nodded my agreement on that one. If she didn't want to go, we couldn't make her. We'd be no better than her mother if we did. And maybe she really was happy there. It sounded like a pretty easy life, even if it wasn't exactly a good one. But the girl never had to work, and it sounded like she had the necessities covered. She wasn't being beaten or starved, which was more than could be said for a lot of the kids in our valley.

And besides, did we really want to mess with a witch? It was none of our business. Why should we interfere?

My brothers didn't want to leave her trapped, though, and I couldn't just let them go and get their asses kicked by a witch. In the end, we decided to go talk to her the next day. If she was happy in her tower, we'd leave her there. If she wasn't, we'd get her down and hide her somewhere safe where her mother wouldn't find her—or us. I knew just the place.

Our king was on the outs with his nephew, who had taken his place while he'd been gone for ten years. When King Owen came back, he'd reclaimed his place, pushing his nephew aside. The guy was chomping at the bit to get his position back, though I didn't really know why. It didn't seem that desirable a role. The king didn't have more than anyone else, and he got blamed for all the ills that befell our people.

I wasn't born of royal blood, so I obviously didn't understand. I did understand enough about politics to know that if Owen was in the witch's good graces, I couldn't hide the girl there. Since Owen and his nephew were feuding, he'd be all too happy to accept the witch's daughter. It wasn't perfect, but it would do for a start.

"There's one more thing," Jack said. "And this one's kinda strange."

"Stranger than what you already told us?" Daniel asked with a grin, obviously not taking our brothers seriously. I'd been wary myself when William had come back with his story, but Jack's was too outrageous to be a lie. Jack might have been a trickster on occasion, but he wasn't that inventive. William, maybe, but not Jack.

"She said she's a shifter," Jack said.

"She's gotta be a witch," William said. "Her mom's a witch."

"What if she's both?" I asked.

They all turned to stare at me, the wheels turning as they put it together. Her mother was tight with King Owen and had been for a long time. It wasn't inconceivable. He had two legitimate daughters, but that didn't mean he didn't have a few illegitimate ones, too. Her mother was obviously batshit crazy, but maybe she hid her away out of shame because she was Owen's mistress. Or maybe she didn't want Owen's wolf wife to get wind of the affair and retaliate.

"That actually makes sense," Jack said slowly. "She said something about waiting for the wolves' Alpha to marry her. If her father once married wolf royalty, maybe he's got plans for her to do the same."

"Then we've definitely got to get her out of there," Jack said.

"Somebody's got a crush," Daniel said, slugging Jack's shoulder.

"I don't have a crush," Jack said. "But she has no idea what any of that means. She's like a small child. If they marry her off to some wolf guy who doesn't even know her…"

"Then it's none of our business," Daniel said. "Unless you want her."

William held his beer aloft. "I want her," he said. "I'll admit it. She's hot as hell with a voice from heaven."

We all laughed, and Daniel started shoving our little brother around playfully. But I didn't miss the scowl Jack aimed his way, or the brooding expression on his face the rest of the evening.

Chapter Ten

Astrid

This time, I didn't tell Mother Dear about my visitor. Part of me didn't want her to know. I didn't know what she'd do to me or to Jack if I told her what had happened. It wasn't just that I felt an inexplicable desire to protect the boy who most definitely had not come to kill me. Some part of me relished this secret, treasured it like I treasured the silky scrap of paper I'd read until the words faded to almost nothing. I thought of what Jack had said, and a smile found my lips as I bent over my sewing.

That's what sixteen-year-old girls do.

I only knew about one sixteen-year-old girl, and she'd never deceived or disobeyed her mother before—at least not in such a devious way. Maybe it was time to start.

"What are you smiling about?"

"Oh," I said, startled out of my thoughts. "Nothing, Mother Dear. Just that I'm happy this quilt is coming along so well. Maybe you can bring it to Father in the winter."

She narrowed her eyes at me, and my heart began to pound. I bent my head, hiding my face as I slipped the needle through the fabric in the tiny stitches I'd perfected over the years, as precise as the machine stitching on the clothes Mother Dear brought home for me.

I had a new shirt now, one that she hadn't brought home. When she wasn't around, I took it out and buried my face in it, inhaling his heady scent until I grew dizzy, and my whole body tingled, and the smile refused to leave my face. It had only been three days, but I couldn't wait to see them again. Every day I sat on the windowsill combing out my hair and hoping they would return.

On the fourth day, the morning after Mother Dear had visited, I heard a call from below that sent my heart racing like the wind. I ran to the window, my bare feet barely touching the floor. Leaning out, I spotted all four of the boys, and my heart filled so full of joy that I nearly exploded.

"I brought all my brothers this time," William yelled, cupping his hands around his mouth.

"Can you haul us up?" Jack yelled.

"Yes," I yelled back, already snatching the bag and tossing it out the window. My heart rose like a bluebird, soaring and singing and wheeling inside my chest. They had come to see me. I had visitors—friends. At long last.

I ran to the wall and took down the gown I'd brought up for just this occasion. I settled it onto the floor and climbed in through the top, pulling it up and buttoning it as I ran to the window. In my excitement, I hauled the basket up as fast as I could, not bothering to be careful of giving a smooth ride. I felt him bang against the wall a few times, but before long, Jack's disheveled head appeared over the sill. He grabbed hold and hopped out of the basket like he had the last time, so buoyant compared to Mother Dear, like he was made of vibrancy and sunshine.

"That must take some serious arm muscles," he said, squeezing my bicep and letting out a low whistle. "Damn, girl. Remind me never to piss you off."

I nodded, my face aching from smiling so hard.

"How are you?" Jack asked, taking my hands and turning them over like he expected it to be written there instead of on my face.

"Good," I said. "I got dressed this time."

"I can see that," he said. "Can't say I don't miss seeing you in my T-shirt."

"I can put it on if you want."

"Nah," he said, squeezing my arm. "Keep it."

"Thank you," I said. "I like the way it smells. I keep it under my pillow and smell it before I go to sleep."

He licked his lip, a funny look coming over his face like he was trying to stop smiling but it just kept getting bigger instead. "Do you now?"

I nodded hard.

"You have no idea how hot that is," he said.

"It's not as hot as this dress," I said. "But Mother Dear says a—a lady should greet her visitors looking her best. I did my hair, too."

"You sure did," he said, admiring the braid wrapped around and around and piled on top of my head.

"Should we bring up your brothers?"

"If we have to," he said with an easy grin.

I took the rope, but he plucked it out of my hands. "Show me how this works, and I'll do it."

"I can do it."

"I know you can," he said. "I felt those guns. But you're used to hauling up one person, and I brought four. I'm not going to make you do the extra work."

It felt strange to stand back and let him work while I only offered a couple pointers, but he seemed happy enough to haul the next two up. William introduced the other blond boy, a thin one with a lopsided grin and shaggy hair who called himself Daniel and kissed my hand before taking the rope from Jack and hauling up the last boy.

When he arrived, he climbed out carefully instead of hopping out like the other three. His eyes did a quick scan of my room before landing on me. His face was strong and solid, with a square jaw and a broad, serious mouth. He was taller than his brothers, at least as tall as Father Dear, and muscular like Jack. But while Jack was all sunshine, he was like moonlight. He had luminous dark bronze hair and eyes like the deer I'd seen through my binoculars—big and round, with a soft wisdom in their depths.

My room suddenly felt very small. I'd never noticed how much space people took up until my tower was full of them. I couldn't decide who to look at. They were all different, and I wanted to study them all. Jack looked comfortable and easy, with his quick smile and crinkling blue eyes aimed at me even as he gestured to his newly-arrived brother.

"This is Evan," he said. "He doesn't talk much."

"Hi," I said, biting at my lip.

"We're here to rescue you," Daniel said with a bow.

"If you want us to," William said. He might have been the plainest of the brothers, but my fascination was no less than for the others. In fact, it made me like him more. He was easy to look at without getting overwhelmed by all the newness. He was not much bigger than me, so he seemed more familiar and less intimidating, and he had a kind, open face that I instantly trusted despite all Mother Dear had told me about boys.

"How are you going to do that?" I asked. "Mother Dear will know if I leave."

"What if we bring you back?" Jack asked. "You can come out and experience the world and go back before she comes home. Then if you decide you'd rather stay here, you don't have to come out again. And if you want to go out there, we can find some way to make it happen."

I looked at him doubtfully. "How will we get back up here? Someone has to be here to pull up the basket."

They all looked at each other.

William scratched the back of his neck. "We should have brought another rope," he said. "We could have made a pulley system."

"I might be able to fly out," Jack said, turning to Evan. "Or maybe you could?"

Evan gave him a look that I knew well. It meant, "Shut up if you know what's good for you." But I was still stuck on Jack's words.

A feeling stirred inside me, this small betrayal enough to cast doubt over all of them, over everything they said. "I thought you were a stag," I said.

Jack turned to me, then drew back when he saw my expression, his eyebrows drawing down. "I am," he said. "That's my natural form. But we're shifters. We can turn into other things with some effort and practice. Flying is one of the hardest things for a land animal shifter, though."

I shook my head, backing away slowly. "No. If you shift into another animal, you'll get stuck that way for the rest of your life. You must never, ever shift into anything but a turtle."

They stared at me as my voice rose.

Evan cocked an eyebrow at me.

"What?" I asked, my breath coming fast from my outburst.

"You're a turtle?" William asked.

"Not what I would have guessed," Daniel said.

"You can shift into anything," Jack said, his brow furrowing as I shook my head harder.

"Don't," I said. "You'll get stuck like that forever."

"Astrid, it's okay," he said. "I promise."

"No," I said. "Don't do it. I'll just stay up here, and you can tell me about the world down there."

While his brothers were looking at me strangely, Jack took my hands in his, gripping my shaking fingers in a steadying hold. "I won't leave you, Astrid."

"Promise?" I asked, my eyes prickling with tears. Crap. That was bad. I couldn't cry in front of them. They'd know my secret.

"Yeah, we've all done it before," William said. "We play as lots of animals when we're kids. Though not birds as often because frankly heights aren't my thing, but I can do a couple other things easily enough. Only werewolves are incapable of using another form. Shifters have a natural form, but we're not bound to one."

"Here, I'll show you," Jack said.

"No," I said, gripping his hands harder. Suddenly, I felt a tear beading on my eyelashes, threatening to fall, and I had to release his hands and lower my face, so he wouldn't see me catch it as it fell.

"Hey," Jack said, sliding an arm around my shoulder. "I'm sorry to say this, but your mother was lying to you. I wouldn't do it if it meant I couldn't come back for you."

I sniffed hard, sucking up all my tears and squeezing my hand closed around the teardrop. "What if Mother Dear put a spell on this place, so it's true up here?" I asked. "What if you get stuck?"

"Shifters don't get stuck," Daniel said.

"They can," I said. "I can make them."

They all stared.

"What?" William asked at last.

I sniffed again, even louder this time. "I can bind a shifter into their form," I said. "So, if they see me when they're in animal form, they can't turn back to human form and tell anyone."

"Shit," Daniel said. "That's some serious paranoia."

"It's not paranoia," I said. "It's protection."

"I'm surprised you know what that means," William said.

"Encyclopedias," I said, gesturing to the bookshelf.

Evan pushed off the windowsill where he'd been leaning and paced the room, frowning.

"Right," Jack said. "Back to the matter at hand. Even if your mom put a spell on this place, she didn't put one on us. As soon as we left, we'd be able to shift back."

I thought about that, and the bird man who had come here. He'd shifted back and forth. But I was still scared for these boys who had come to help me when I didn't even know I needed help. I hadn't known them long, but I already adored every one of them. They weren't just my friends. They were my boys.

Chapter Eleven

Astrid

With an impatient sigh, Evan peeled off his shirt, revealing a tanned expanse of muscle across his chest. He was taller and broader than Jack, but every bit as fascinating. He caught me staring and paused with his hand curled around the button of his jeans.

"He ain't scared of your mother," Daniel said.

"I don't know about this," William asked. "I mean, have you ever seen a guy naked?"

"I saw you," I said.

Daniel hooted and pounded on William's back. "You didn't tell us that!"

"I was in the vines outside," William said. "She didn't see anything."

"She's never even seen a boy in the flesh before us," Jack said. "Obviously she's never seen one naked."

"She did say she had books," William said. "You never know what kind."

"We're just shifting," Daniel said. "It's not like we're pervy guys flashing our junk at her."

"What junk?" I asked.

They all exchanged a look, and I got the feeling I was missing out on something.

"What?" I asked. Mother Dear had always told me to wear clothes, scolding me when she came home to find me without. But I didn't see why it mattered. I liked to be comfortable. But obviously it mattered a lot, because every time these boys talked about it, they got strange looks on their faces.

"So, like, do you know what sex is?" Daniel asked.

"Dude," Jack said, shooting Daniel a warning look.

"No," I said. "What is it?"

"Your mother couldn't have given you the S encyclopedia," William muttered.

"I never thought I'd be having this conversation before I hit twenty," Jack said with a sigh.

"Even if you were a dad before twenty, you wouldn't be having this conversation for a long time," Daniel said.

"So, what is it?" I asked.

Jack rubbed his hair, messing up the curls. "It's, like, when your bodies join together, and, uh…"

The other three were snorting with suppressed laughter.

"And what?" I asked, folding my arms over my chest.

Jack glared at his brothers. "Help me out here?"

Daniel cleared his throat. "When a man and a woman love each other very much…"

This time, they all started laughing.

I stamped my foot. "Why are you laughing at me? I can't help it that I don't know what goes on out there in your world. So, let's have it."

"Let's have sex?" Daniel asked, and they all burst out laughing again.

"You better stop laughing right now," I said, shaking a finger at them. "Or I'll…I'll…hang you out the window by your toes."

That only made them laugh harder. I crossed my arms and turned my back to them. Maybe I should have dumped hot water on them like Mother Dear instructed.

"Sorry," Jack said, coming up behind me and putting a hand on my shoulder. "It's not you. It's just kind of awkward, that's all."

"Are you going to tell me or laugh at me some more?"

"We'll tell you," William said.

"Come on," Jack said, tugging at my shoulder.

I let him turn me around.

"It's kind of a big deal," he said. "To people out there."

"Not to you?" I asked.

"No, it is," he said quickly. "To us, too."

"Why is it a big deal?"

"Because… Because that's how you get a baby. If you want one."

"I don't want a baby," I said. "I've never even set foot outside my tower."

"You don't have to have a baby from it," William said. "Only if you want."

"Okay," I said. "If I don't want a baby, is it still a big deal?"

"Yeah," Jack said. "It is."

I still didn't understand what it was. "Why?"

"I…I'm not sure," Jack said, looking to his brothers for help.

"Because it feels so good," Daniel said.

"Show me how."

Jack's eyes went shiny, and he pressed his lips together, and I knew he was trying not to laugh. "It's, uh, a special thing."

"And that's bad?"

"Some people think you should only share it with your husband when you're married," William said. "And it's bad if you do it before that."

"Oh." I thought about that a minute and then asked, "Do you think that?"

"No," all four of them said in unison.

I blinked at them. "Why do other people think that?"

"Because, um…" William started.

"It feels too good," Daniel said. "And they're afraid everyone will run around doing it all the time."

"And that girls will accidentally get pregnant," Jack added.

"It will be harder for adults to control us," Daniel said.

"Some people think it's a sacred ritual," Jack said. "And it's too important to be shared with just anyone."

"Oh," I said, finally starting to understand. "Like treasure."

They all stopped talking to look at me.

"Treasure can't be shared with just anyone," I said. "I'm only supposed to share it with the prince once we get married, and even then, he's not supposed to know about all my treasure. I only give him a little."

"That's sex," Daniel said.

"No, it's treasure. I can show you."

William's cheeks turned pink, and he swallowed. He had that lump on his throat, too.

"Astrid," Jack said, his eyes shining with laughter in that way that made me feel all warm and smiley, too. "That's what your mother was talking about when she called it treasure. She was talking about your body. About sex."

I nodded, but it didn't really make sense. Treasure came from my eyes, not my body. But it had never made sense to me. Pretty things were pretty, but nothing more. Mother Dear told me they were valuable, but I didn't know how treasure was better than a bird soaring over the valley, or a flower in the meadow below, or rain dripping past my window. I was tired of having all this treasure and not knowing what it meant.

"Have you done sex?" I asked.

Three of them nodded. William shook his head.

"Wait a minute," Daniel said, turning to William. "You said Marla—."

"Shut up, okay?" William said, his skin going pink shade all the way to his ears this time. "She didn't want to."

"You could have told us," Jack said.

William hung his head. "I didn't want to look like a loser."

"Oh, man," Daniel said. "You definitely need to get laid."

"Me, too," I said.

They all stared at me a second, and then three of them burst into laughter. Evan shook his head with a small smile.

"What?" I asked. "I don't want to look like a loser, either."

Daniel smacked himself in the forehead with his palm. "I knew we'd explain it badly."

"If we both need to do this…" William started.

Jack held up a hand. "Oh, no," he said. "If anyone touches her, it's someone who knows what he's doing. At least the first time."

"Yeah, okay," William said. "You're right."

Evan stepped over to place both hands on my shoulders. "You don't look like a loser." He gave me this look that made me so dizzy I had to grip the floor with my toes, so I wouldn't fall over. "You're beautiful."

"Devastatingly beautiful," Jack said.

"Irresistible," William said, nodding.

"Drop dead gorgeous," Daniel said.

"I know," I said.

Evan stepped back, and they all did that thing where they stared at me with their mouths hanging open.

"I'm the second most beautiful girl in the world," I said.

"Second?" Jack asked, cocking an eyebrow, a smile twitching at the corner of his lips. "Don't get too humble now."

"I'm second after Mother Dear," I said. "I could be first, but my hair isn't golden like hers."

Evan dropped his head into his hands, shaking it slowly back and forth.

"Okay, let's drop the sex talk and get back to shifting," Jack said. "Usually, you'll be somewhat close to what your parents were. Like, I'm a deer, Evan's a horse, and William here is a cow."

"A bull," William said, glaring.

"I'm a dog," Daniel said. "Trust me when I say it's hard to live that one down when it comes to the ladies."

"Always chasing tail," Jack said with a grin. "Even when he has to chase his own."

"That's not close to the others," I said. "That's not even an herbivore."

"She knows that, but not how babies are made," William said, shaking his head.

"I got the dog from my mom," Daniel said.

"Mother Dear isn't a shifter," I said.

"But your father is," Jack said. "He's actually the king of the shifters. Right?"

"You know?" I whispered, panic rising inside me. Somehow, they knew who I was. Maybe that's why they'd come to get me. They knew I was the shifter princess, and they wanted to steal me away. I squeezed my hand shut around the treasure.

"We figured your dad was King Owen," Daniel said, like it didn't matter at all, like it wasn't even important. It wasn't something to say in hushed tones or hide. He went right on musing about how Father Dear was a big cat, so that meant there was a ninety percent chance that I was actually a feline of some sort or at least a big predator. Like that was more important than the fact that I was a princess with a room full of treasure below me. These boys weren't here to steal my treasure. They didn't even care. They cared more about freeing me.

It made me wonder what else Mother Dear had lied about. It made me wonder what was out there that she had tried so hard to keep me from.

"Wait," I said. "I've only been a turtle. Are you saying that's not what I really am?"

"That's what we're saying," Jack said with a grin that was so filled with excitement that it made my own about-to-lose-it feeling settle. "If you've never tried to be anything else, how do you know what you are naturally?"

"Because…because that's what I chose?"

"You don't choose," William said. "It comes out as you learn to shift. It's effortless, and you feel a connection with that animal in the wild. And when you're in that form, it's like you're complete in a whole new way. You feel…calm. Everything just is. You don't question things. There's no confusion."

I thought of the struggle to turn into a turtle, how it hurt and took endless concentration and sometimes, pain. Mother Dear didn't like me to shift, and I didn't like it, either, so I rarely did it. It felt nothing like what he described. I tried to think of what would make me feel like that. When I saw the birds soaring over the mountains, I felt peaceful, but not in the way he described. They filled my heart with such longing I sometimes felt like I'd die, like my heart would beat its wings until it tore through my ribcage and out the window to join them.

But I wasn't a bird. Maybe if I saw a big cat, I would feel the same about them. Maybe I'd feel even more strongly connected, and I wouldn't feel the longing to be free. I'd only feel the peacefulness.

"Can you take me to see Father Dear?" I asked.

They broke off talking. Evan raised his eyebrows in a question, his gaze so intense it made me squirm. "Does he know you're here?"

"Of course."

"We were afraid of that," Daniel said, sinking onto the edge of my bed.

"We can take you," Jack said slowly. "But chances are, he wouldn't like that. If he knows you're here, he wants you here as much as your mother. We just don't know exactly why."

"I know why," I said. The answer was pressing into my palm. But I needed more answers than that. I needed a better reason than a shiny teardrop. Even a thousand tiny teardrops weren't enough to explain why I hadn't had friends like this my whole life.

"Why?" Evan asked.

I shook my head. "I can't tell you."

"Okay, so who wants to shift into a bird?" Jack asked. "I'm pretty confident that I can make it from here to the ground, at least."

My hand turned into a fist around the treasure. I had always done what Mother Dear said. When she said I had to be a turtle, I'd believed her. I'd been a turtle. Now these boys were telling me I had to be a cat, but I wasn't a cat, either. I didn't care what my father was, or what my mother was, or where treasure came from. I tossed it onto the bed and pulled my purple gown from my shoulders, dropping it to the floor.

"I'll do it."

Chapter **Twelve**

Astrid

Four sets of eyes glued to me like I was made of treasure, like my body really was treasure. Like I wasn't the second-most beautiful girl in the world. Like I was more than a girl, or a turtle, or a shifter, or even a princess. Like I was…me.

"Whoa," Daniel whispered.

"Do what?" Jack asked, his voice kind of choked.

I imagined the birds I'd seen, the peace eagles and the crows, the blackbirds and hawks. I threw my arms up, and a prickling sensation rippled across my skin. Power surged through my body, a hundred times greater than thunder rolling through the clouds in a storm. As it grew inside me, I seemed to shrink externally. I looked up, gasping at the feathers spreading along my arms. No, not arms. I was spread wide, admiring my giant red-gold wings. I was no turtle, no fox, and no cat. I was a bird.

And then I fell to the floor.

Relief like I'd never felt before rippled through me, and I beat my wings, but nothing happened. I beat them harder, batting them against the floor until feathers started coming loose.

"Stop," Jack said, crouching next to me. Dust swirled under the bed. I looked up at Jack. The boys were staring at me.

"Can you shift back?" William asked, falling to his knees beside Jack.

"Guess you always knew you weren't a turtle," Daniel said, sitting on his heels and running a hand over my feathered back.

Evan crouched, too, holding out a hand to me.

I didn't want to be a human in a cage. I wanted to be a bird, flying free through the spring sunshine. But since I didn't know how, I thought of my human body. Of the feeling of Jack's skin under my fingertips, the rush of warm over my bare skin when he looked at me. A second later, I shifted back and found myself standing in the center of a circle boys.

None of them rose. Evan and Jack, who were sitting on their heels, dropped their knees to the floor. My eyes moved from one to the next. William, with his curious eyes peering out from behind his glasses, who had told his brothers I was here in the first place. Daniel, with his quick laughter and jokes. Evan, who had barely spoken since he was here but whose eyes made me shiver with sensations I didn't understand. And Jack, with his bright yellow curls and his smile that could calm me when I started to freak out. They were all serious now, all staring at me with identical expressions of wonder and awe. Expressions that said I was a princess, and they would worship me if that was what I wanted.

But I didn't want that. Not from them. Maybe some of what Mother Dear said was true. My father was the shifter king. One day, I would be the queen. Right now, though, I was just me, and I didn't want these boys to treat me as if I were anything else. They weren't here to steal from me or hurt me. They were here to set me free.

"Why can't I fly?" I asked.

"You haven't practiced," William said. "Birds aren't born knowing how to fly."

"Who can teach me?"

Evan's eyes locked on mine, and he gave the slightest nod.

"Okay," I said. "Come back tomorrow."

"Don't you want to go outside now?" Daniel asked, rising to his feet. "We can lower you in the basket."

"No," I said. "When I leave, I want to fly out on my own wings."

"Are you sure?" Jack asked, reaching up to take my hand. "It might take a while."

"That's okay," I said. "I've been waiting sixteen years. I'm a patient girl."

I didn't say the last part. That I needed time to get ready, to prepare myself. Because when I flew out of there, I was never coming back.

Chapter Thirteen

Astrid

That evening, as I sat on my windowsill, I wondered where Mother Dear had gone in the world today. What had she seen and done that was so terrible that I couldn't see and do the same things? She must have been protecting me from something out there. But if it was so horrible, why could she face it day after day while I had to stay here?

It could be that I was weak and stupid, as she'd always told me, but I didn't believe that anymore. At least, I was starting to question it. The boys didn't make me feel weak and stupid. They looked at me like I was a goddess. They made me feel powerful and incredible.

And what could be more horrible than being trapped up here my whole life, being told I was too special for the world? I didn't want to be special. I just wanted to be Astrid, the girl, the bird. Not a turtle who would get stuck as an animal forever if I tried to change into something else, so I must never, ever try. I'd been trapped here not by my body or this tower but by her words—her lies.

I could have flown out of here all along. What could be more horrible than knowing that?

I waited until I grew sleepy under the full moon, but Mother Dear did not come. I heard wolves howling down in the Second Valley. On the other side of my mountain, the First Valley was filled with witches I'd never met. Witches who I'd been told wanted my treasure—but did they? If Mother Dear had lied to me about who I was, what I was, why should I believe anything she said?

In the morning, the sky was dark and heavy with rain. I kicked off the blanket and went to the window, my heart sinking when raindrops began to streak past. Mother Dear hadn't come the night before, and she rarely came during the day, so I couldn't demand explanations. And Evan wouldn't come all the way here in the rain. I sat on the sill, watching the dreary weather that matched my mood. It seemed impossible that only a month had passed since the eclipse. Only a month ago, I'd been happy enough in my tower all alone.

I'd been impatient to get down and start living the life Mother Dear had always promised for me, but that was all. It had been a vague dissatisfaction. Now that I'd experienced just a few days of the people out there, I couldn't go back. I hadn't even found freedom, and already I knew I could never be happy in my cage again.

A few hours later, as I was sitting before the mirror singing, I heard steady hoofbeats approaching. My hairbrush clattered to the surface of the vanity, my heart pounding harder than the horse's hooves. I raced to the window just as a sheet of rain blew in, soaking me. I barely felt it. Laughing with joy, I threw down the basket without waiting for him to appear. And then he did, a big, dark stallion racing along the path and bursting into my clearing.

He shifted and jumped into the basket without checking to make sure it was really me up here. I hadn't bothered with clothes that morning, and I didn't bother with them now. I pulled him up, hand over hand, until the basket reached the window. I reached out, gripping his upper arms, and he slid into the room with me, both of us wet from the torrents of rain sluicing down from the sky.

We were both breathing hard—him from running and me from hauling up the basket as fast as I could. Our bodies were close, close enough that I could feel the heat of his body despite his cold skin. Water trickled from his dark hair down his sculpted cheekbones and jaw, dripping onto his broad shoulders and trickling down the ridges of hard muscle of his chest and abs.

"Oh," I breathed as my eyes dropped lower. "What's that?"

"That's what a boy looks like naked," he said, his voice low and husky.

"All boys have an extra limb?" I asked. "What's it for? Does it help you climb?"

"No," he said, a small smile on his lips.

"What's funny?"

He cleared his throat. "It's for sex."

I tried to remember exactly what they'd said about sex being related to treasure. "It gives you treasure?"

"It gets me treasure," Evan said, still smiling a little.

"How?" I asked, suspicion rising. "Is it like a hand that grabs treasure?"

A small chuckle escaped him. "Sort of."

"Does it suck it up like an anteater?"

"No," he said, his smile dropping away. "It goes inside you."

I stared at the limb that was starting to grow up toward me. I stepped back, even more wary now. Now it looked the way I imagined snakes looked—rising slowly to strike. Transfixed, I waited for him to do something with it. At last, the words burst out of me. "What's it doing?" I asked, my voice sounding high and a bit panicked. "Why's it growing?"

Evan cocked an eyebrow. "Because you're paying attention to it. You don't want it to get bigger?"

"There's no way that can fit in my eye!"

Evan choked on a bubble of laughter. "Your eye?"

"Treasure comes from my eyes," I said. "You can't put that in my eye."

"No," Evan said. "It goes...you know. Between your legs."

"Promise?"

"I promise," Evan said, still smirking. "I will never put it in your eye."

"When does it stop growing?" I asked, relaxing a little. It was very interesting. It looked like it was almost twice as big as when he started, growing up like the vines on the side of the tower.

"Uh... It gets a little bigger."

"Can I touch it?" I asked, remembering how it felt to touch Jack, how soft his skin had been.

Evan swallowed. He had that thing in his throat, too. I wondered if all boys had it. Father Dear had a beard, so I had never seen his throat bared. Now I wondered how many other secrets boys had that I didn't know about. Maybe they kept their treasure in a pouch in their throats like a bird's gullet.

"If you want," he said. "But you should know it, uh, feels really good when you touch it."

I nodded, edging forward until I could reach him. I poked it with one finger, then jerked back.

"It won't hurt you," he said. "You don't have to do anything you don't want. And you can stop whenever you feel like it. You're safe. I promise."

I nodded harder, biting my lip as I reached for it again. It was both harder and softer than I'd imagined. His skin was much softer than Jack's, and so, so warm. "Oh," I whispered. "That does feel good."

Evan nodded, squeezing his eyes closed, fisting his hands at his sides.

I pulled back. "Oh, no. Did I hurt you?"

He shook his head, swallowing so loud I could hear it.

"What's wrong?"

"Nothing," he said. "You can explore and satisfy your curiosity. But then don't ever do this to someone you don't, uh, have feelings for."

"What sort of feelings? I asked. "I have lots of feelings about you. I like you because you're nice, and you came even though it was raining. I have curious feelings and exciting feelings."

"I like you, too," he said. "You're strangely endearing."

I swallowed, stepping close again. I could smell the rain, both on him and outside. I moved closer, so more of my body could touch his. Strange feelings stirred inside me, and my heart began to beat harder. My hands moved up his torso, over the muscles that bunched under my hands, his arms that started out brown at his hands and grew lighter as I moved up to his shoulders. A scattering of brown freckles dotted his shoulders. I wanted to count them, to kiss them, to map them like the stars in the constellations.

My skin shivered, but inside I felt hot, almost unbearably so. Something inside me was waking up, lifting its head and uncoiling like a snake. I leaned in, laying my cheek on his chest, lifting my face to inhale the scent of his neck. It curled through me like Jack's had, awakening the beast further. I imagined that snake moving faster, flicking its tongue out. I stuck my tongue out and caught a drop of water running down Evan's chest, his cold skin prickling under my warm tongue.

He sucked in a breath and shuddered, his body pressing insistently against mine. The heat of his core melded with mine, and that nameless need in my center called for more. I had never touched a boy before, and I wanted to keep touching. I wanted to wrestle him on the ground, roll our bodies together like the people I'd seen in the field that way. This wasn't close enough. Nothing would be close enough until I sucked him in through my skin and absorbed him.

"You can touch me, too," I whispered, taking his hands from his sides and putting them on me like I had Jack's. Evan didn't hesitate like his brother had. His hands moved over me in long, deep strokes, each one kindling the fire inside me until I was buzzing with a frantic need.

"More," I whispered.

He clamped his hands around my waist, lifting me onto the windowsill where I'd sat a thousand nights waiting for a prince to come and tell me it was time. No prince had come for me, telling me he would take me away and make me his princess. Instead, an ordinary shifter had come, and now he stood between my knees, his neck arched as he bent to bury his face in my shoulder. He tugged my hair until my head dropped back, and his mouth skimmed along my throat. Sparks exploded behind my eyelids, rushing through my limbs like the streams that ran down the mountain after a downpour.

His lips pressed against my skin, hard at first and then softer, then hard again. His hand slid behind me, cradling my body as his mouth moved lower, pushing me back over the drop below. He held me gently even as his mouth ravaged my skin, drawing it up between his teeth, sucking me with his lips, then tasting with his tongue. I clung to him, my legs and arms wrapping around him, trusting my body to him fully. The drop would kill me, but I had no fear. He would never let me go.

And I would never be satisfied until I'd devoured him, consumed him the way the need he'd planted inside me was consuming me. The pressure built between my legs until it was an ache, and I pressed against him, trying to find relief. But it wasn't enough. I thought maybe I wasn't a bird at all but a carnivore, some kind of giant cat like my father, a lioness hungry for this boy's flesh.

"More," I said again, wrenching at his shoulders.

"I can't," he said, pressing his forehead against the center of my chest. His breath was quick against my skin.

"Why?" I demanded, though I didn't know what he couldn't do.

"I don't have a condom," he said, his voice half words and half groan.

"What's that?"

"To make sure we're safe," he said.

"From what?" I asked, glancing over my shoulder. All I saw was rain and the valley below, the same thing I'd seen for sixteen years. I wanted something different. I wanted more of what he'd shown me.

"Safe from getting pregnant," he said. "From having a baby."

"You did something to me." I gripped his arms and stared into his eyes. "You made this happen. Now make it stop."

His hands fell to my waist, and he took a deep breath, leaning in to run his cheek slowly over mine. "Okay," he said, his voice going husky again. "Okay. I can help you out. If you're sure it's what you want."

"I'm sure," I said.

He closed his eyes and moved his cheek against mine, little prickles scratching softly over my smooth skin as his cold hand moved up my warm thigh. I gasped at the incredible sensation when he touched me, his fingers moving slowly at first, teasing me, winding me tighter and tighter. At last, though, he pushed harder against me, pushing until the tension broke and waves of heat rushed through my body.

Stars bloomed into suns behind my eyelids, and my blood shimmered like those suns had all hit the wet world below at once.

I came back into my body slowly, not like when Mother Dear made me go out, so she could practice using my body, and when I came back into it, I was snapped like a rubber band. This time I oozed into my body languidly, liquidly. Evan's fingers dug into my hipbone, and he was breathing so fast against my neck I thought he might faint.

"Are you okay?" I whispered.

"Are you?" he asked, not lifting his head. "Did I hurt you? You made that sound…"

"Hurt me? No," I breathed, burying my hands in his dark hair. "I've never felt anything like that in my life. What just happened?"

He chuckled, drawing away slowly. "That's what sex is like. Only everything is…bigger."

"Let's do it."

"I'll bring a condom next time," he said. "Now, we fly."

Chapter Fourteen

Astrid

An hour later, I hated Evan so much I was contemplating pushing him out the window. He'd started by shifting into a bird and trying to show me how to fly, though he could only do it for a minute before he had to sit down. I had tried and promptly fallen to the floor. He'd shifted back into human form, lifted me up to the top of my vanity, and told me to try again.

Again, I had crashed in a heap to the floor. He picked me up and put me back on the vanity. "Try again," he said. "And flap your wings this time."

I crashed to the floor, flapping my wings all the way.

He picked me up and set me back. "Again."

I fell.

He picked me up.

I fell.

He picked me up.

I refused to jump.

He crossed his arms and cocked an eyebrow. "You're going to live here for the next sixteen years?"

I opened my beak and screeched at him.

He laughed. Then, he pushed me off.

I flopped to the floor. Feathers flew up from my bruised body.

He picked me up.

I pecked him.

He grabbed me around the neck with one hand and the feet with the other, holding me up to his face. "I've wrung enough chickens' necks in my life," he said. "I don't think you want to do that."

I beat my wings furiously, wanting to peck his eyes out.

A slow smirk tugged at his lips. "Keep flapping like that, and you'll be flying in no time."

He threw me. I hurtled across the room, flapping until I hit the wall. Then I crashed to the floor again.

Evan bent, his hands on his knees. "Ready to give up already?"

I dragged my body up, though I was sure one of my wings was broken. I shifted into human form, breathing hard as I lay curled on the wooden floorboards. "Go away."

"Did you think this would be easy?"

"Yes," I said, cradling my arm. I was too tired and battered to pretend. I'd been watching birds all my life. They made it look more than easy. They flew effortlessly, without even flapping.

"It's been an hour," Evan said. "You spent sixteen years with your feet on the ground."

"I'd rather be a turtle," I said.

"Then be one," he said. "No one is stopping you. I'm not going to make you fly. It's up to you, Astrid. Do you want to fly or not?"

"Not," I moaned.

"Suit yourself," Evan said, straightening. "Come visit me when you change your mind."

With that, he turned into a bird and flapped hard until he lifted off. I took great satisfaction in his misjudgment of my window. He clipped a wing on one side of it, losing a few feathers in the process. I lay on the floor catching my breath until I heard hoofbeats racing off down the mountain. Then I dragged myself up, shifted into a bird, and tried again.

The next morning, when I sat in my window combing my hair, my mind returned to Evan. I could still smell him, could feel his mouth on my skin and his fingers relieving my unbearable longing. I shivered at the memory. He'd lit a spark within me, but it needed him the way fire needed oxygen to burn. I closed my eyes, running the comb from the crown of my head down as far as I could reach. My lips parted, and I began to sing.

When I opened my eyes, I gasped. The rain had stopped, and the sun shone full and bright on the dripping, dead leaves of the vines. But amid the drooping brown leaves, I saw new green buds pushing up toward the sun. Mother Dear must not have cut through the vines completely, and somehow, they had revived in the rain. They had revived with my song.

And even though Evan had said he wouldn't return, hope bloomed in my chest. With the vines there, I didn't feel so alone anymore. The tiny buds shone like a promise, bright and full of life, inviting me to come out and play.

"Just a little higher," I said to them. "Either you will reach my window, or I'll learn to fly."

From that day on, each morning I sat in the window combing my hair and singing to the vines. And each day, they grew. I didn't wait for them, though. Instead of reading my books or working on my quilt, I practiced my flight. I tried and tried, falling until my feathers were scraggly and my body one big bruise layered upon more bruises.

One day, I would do it. I would learn, and I would fly down into the Third Valley and find Evan and peck every hair from his head and every freckle from his shoulders. I would go to see Father Dear and ask him how he could let Mother Dear do this to me. I would find her and see what she did all day. I would fly circles around Daniel and Jack, showing off my red-gold wings and my fierce talons. I would sing to William, who had fallen in love with my song. But first, I had to fly.

Days passed, and I began to think the boys had all left, that none of them would come back. And then one day I heard a voice outside again. When I looked out, I found Daniel at the top of the vine, only half a dozen feet from my window.

"Hello, gorgeous," he said, grinning up at me with such a smile that I couldn't resist returning it. With one smile, my sorrow and frustration and anger melted away.

"You came," I cried, tossing the basket to him.

"I never miss a chance," he said, grabbing onto the basket. He didn't bother to climb inside, just held on while I hauled him up. We stood surveying each other. Today we both wore clothes—he had on jeans and a blue T-shirt, and I wore a simple cotton slip dress.

"I can fly," I said, unable to stop smiling. "A little."

"Yeah?" he asked, cocking his head to one side. "Let's see it."

I bit my lip, shy suddenly. What if he made fun of me for my tiny bit of progress? But I was proud of what I'd accomplished, even if it wasn't much, and I wanted to share it with someone.

"I don't have to look," he said, turning away. He'd mistaken my hesitance for fear of him seeing me without clothes. Suddenly, I remembered the way he'd looked at me when I had shifted into my animal form the first time. When I'd turned back to human, he'd gazed at me with such reverence I had felt taller than the vine outside, more invincible, as boundless as the sky overhead and the mountains below.

I slipped my arms from my dress and let the purple fabric drop to the floor, puddling around my feet. "You can look."

"Really?" He turned around with a grin on his face. It slipped as his eyes drank in every inch of my skin.

"Yes."

I wanted him to watch me forever. I climbed onto the bed, noting the way his eyes widened and his throat moved as he swallowed. Then, I shifted into my favorite bird—a brilliant auburn falcon the same color as my hair. For some reason, his adoration seemed to dim a bit. I spread my wings and beat at the air, commanding his admiration.

"Damn, girl," Daniel said with a laugh. "You look fierce as fuck."

I didn't know how fierce fuck was, but his tone said it was pretty fierce, so I was appeased. I leapt off the bed and swooped all the way to the wall before I turned and continued around the room.

"That's amazing," Daniel cried, clapping his hands together.

I circled the room twice more before plowing into the bed, rolling across the blankets in a flurry of wings, and thudding to a stop against the wall. I quickly shifted back, sitting up and smoothing the blanket. "I'm having some trouble figuring out the landing."

Daniel just gaped at me with his mouth hanging open in a huge smile that did look a lot like the pictures of dogs I'd seen. "You learned that in a week?" he asked.

I nodded, pride swelling my heart even bigger.

He grabbed my hands and pulled me to my feet. I could have stopped myself, but I fell against him instead. I hadn't forgotten how incredible it felt to have my body pressed against another person's. He wrapped his arms tightly around me, lifted me off my feet, and spun me around and around and around. My feet flew out behind me, and laughter bounced off the walls to the room. I was so happy my heart felt like it had wings of its own, like it could soar up and up into the sky above.

Daniel's laughter was different than mine and Mother Dear's. It was big and booming, deeper than mine. Instead of burying mine as Mother Dear's high, tinkling laughter did, his seemed to boost my sweet, bubbling laugh, magnifying it so it was as big as his, mingling with it so it was half of something new that was neither mine nor his. The sound of our laughs braided together to form a song that had never been sung before. Our song.

Chapter Fifteen

Astrid

At last, Daniel set me down, his eyes shining as if his joy had filled his body all the way up until it spilled out through his eyes.

"Your eyes," I said, taking his face between my hands. "They're the color of treasure."

Daniel pulled his lips in, so I couldn't see them anymore. I could see that he was trying not to smile, though. I tilted his face back and forth, staring at his red-gold eyes. They were darker than treasure, but close enough in color. I didn't know eyes could be that color. My eyes were blue or grey depending on the light of that day or what I wore. Mother Dear had blue eyes, or sometimes brown or green if she'd brought home another body. I didn't know someone could have treasure right there in his eyes, not leaking out.

"You mean this?" Daniel asked at last, his fingers skimming across my smooth belly and sinking lower, barely brushing across the tuft of hair where my thighs met. Tingles exploded through my body, sweeping goosebumps across my skin.

"No," I whispered, stepping closer, pressing my hips against his. "Treasure."

"Everyone's always told me they're the color of whiskey," he said, smiling down at me as his hands slid around my hips. "But I like your version better."

"Really?"

"Yeah," he said, his hands cupping my bottom, sending waves of pleasure racing through me. "Treasure makes me think of you."

My heart skipped in my chest, and I swallowed hard. "Why?" I whispered.

"Because you're a treasure," he said. "Your mom's the dragon hoarding you for herself instead of sharing you with the world."

I relaxed. He didn't know. None of them knew, and they still liked me.

"What's whiskey?" I asked as Daniel ran his hands up my back.

"Whiskey's a drink that makes me think of my old man, and I don't like him so much. He dumped us on Evan and Will's mom and took off."

"I won't do that," I said, slipping my arms around his neck.

"I didn't think so." Daniel smiled, stroking his fingertips up and down my back until my whole body was alive, trembling for more, and that ravenous, wild hunger raged inside me. I wanted to grab him and throw him on the bed, roll in him the way I'd wanted to roll in Evan. I leaned in, pressing my nose behind his ear and inhaling as long and deep as I could. He smelled like Evan and Jack, and not like them at the same time. He smelled like grass and that salty, mouthwatering smell that they all had, the heady scent of boy.

I pressed my nose against the crook between his neck and shoulder, breathing him in. Then I tasted him. His skin was saltier than Evan's, and without the tang of rain.

"What was that?" he asked, his hands stilling on my back, cradling the bottom of my ribcage.

"I wanted to know what you taste like," I said, my mouth still grazing his skin.

His hands tightened, pulling me closer. "Can I see what you taste like?"

I nodded, letting my own hands run down over his small, hard shoulders and the ropey muscles of his arms. He scooped me up in one swift movement, so suddenly it made a little cry escape my lips. Daniel laughed and lay me back on the bed. He gave me a wicked grin that made the flame inside me flicker and tremble. "Prepare to be tasted."

He started at the base of my throat, where I'd tasted his skin, and moved down my body. I'd never realized how much sensation was hiding in my body, dormant like the falcon that had hidden inside me for all those years. It was as if I'd thought my body was only a vessel for my soul, the way my tower was a house for my body. Now, I found out I was so much more.

Just like his mouth was so much more than just something to eat or talk with. It was lips for tugging, a tongue for tasting, teeth for teasing, breath for caressing. It was a tool for exploring, for finding new territories that had never been claimed. But he didn't just discover me. He awakened me. With each breath against my skin, he breathed soul into my body, until every inch of me was alive, vibrating with energy, life, and pleasure. As he worshipped each inch of my body that no one had ever noticed, he swept away the ashes and fanned the coals inside me until they were flames raging to consume.

When at last he brought me the same relief Evan had, I couldn't tell if he'd devoured me or I'd devoured him. I just knew that my hunger had been sated.

Daniel sat back on his heels from where he'd been kneeling beside the bed, his grin firmly in place. His attention flickered, and he bent and plucked something off the floor under the edge of the bed. "You lost an earring," he said, holding out his fingers.

When I reached out automatically, he dropped one of my tears into my palm. I snapped my hand closed around it, my heart racing. I knew where it had come from. I'd thrown it on the bed the first time I shifted, and I hadn't thought of it again until this very moment. Mother Dear would kill me if she knew. And these boys, would they still like me just the same if they knew what I could do? Mother Dear always told me people would exploit my gift, and though I didn't think the boys would, they might see me differently. They might not see me as just a simple girl, as simply me, if they knew that I could give them so much treasure they'd never want for anything again.

Before either of us could speak, I heard a sound that doused my fiery blood like a bucket of water in winter.

"Oh, Astrid," Mother Dear trilled from outside the tower. "I'm home."

"Oh shit," Daniel said, jumping to his feet. "Is that your mom?"

I jumped up and grabbed Daniel, dragging him to the edge of the carpet. I threw it back and yanked up the hatch. "Go down," I hissed.

"I just did," Daniel said with a sloppy grin.

"Hurry," I said, pushing him to the opening. He swung his legs into the darkness and started down.

"Throw down the basket," Mother Dear called. "I don't have all day."

119

I didn't have time for Daniel to climb down the ladder, so I eased the hatch closed, replaced the carpet, and raced to the window, my heart beating faster than Evan's horse hooves.

"Coming," I called, dropping the basket out the window. I glanced back over my shoulder and caught a glint of the teardrop I'd let fall back on the bed. Mother Dear would be furious to find a piece of treasure lying around. That always brought with it a punishment that produced another flood of treasure.

Mother Dear yanked on the rope, and I started pulling her up. Then I saw my dress still pooled on the floor where I'd left it when I shifted.

"My dress," I gasped. I was already holding the rope, so I couldn't go and grab it, but I couldn't leave it in the middle of the floor. Mother Dear would wonder why I'd gotten dressed and then undressed in the same day. Before I had thought of a solution, Mother Dear had arrived, pulling up to the window and holding out an arm so I could help her inside. I maneuvered us around to face the basket while we took out her bags.

"I'm sorry I haven't been around," she said. "It's been a busy week."

"What were you doing?" I asked, trying to sound casual. If I could hold it in, if I could make her think everything was okay, maybe Daniel would be okay. He might be downstairs a while, but when she left, he could escape. I gulped at the thought of what I'd done. He was downstairs. Down there. With all my treasure exposed.

He would know what I had, what I was.

"Oh, you know," Mother Dear said.

"No, actually I don't," I said, unable to hold in a little of my bitterness.

Mother Dear turned to me, her eyes narrowed. "What's gotten into you this year?" she asked. "You've been nothing but insolent since the eclipse. Am I not doing everything in my power to make you a queen for the rest of your life?"

I didn't know what she was doing anymore. I didn't even know if I wanted to be queen. It was something hypothetical that I didn't fully understand, though I'd read it in a hundred stories. Mother Dear had prepared me for this my whole life, and I'd always known it was my destiny. I didn't know if I was being a coward now or if my eyes had finally been opened, but all I wanted to do was run away with my boys and never have to see this room again.

"And what have I told you about leaving your clothes lying around?" Mother Dear said, marching over to my dress.

My heart stopped.

"Sorry, sorry," I said, rushing across the room to grab up my dress. I ran to the wall and hung my dress.

She stared at me so long I wondered if she could see my visitors on me like some kind of mark. "Don't you think you should put that on instead of hanging it up?"

Crap. I'd been too nervous to think about getting dressed, and now I'd acted funny. I quickly pulled the dress over my head, apologizing all the while.

Mother Dear gave a sniff, the corners of her mouth pulling down. "This must be the first time you haven't asked me how long I'm staying," she said. "I don't know if I'm more hurt that you haven't missed me or relieved that you're finally growing less annoying." She gave a high laugh to show me she was kidding, but I wasn't so sure anymore.

In truth, I hadn't missed Mother Dear. I'd worried she'd come home and find me shifting, yes, but I hadn't longed to see her walking through the woods, to hear her voice calling my name. I'd missed the boys I had just met more than the mother I'd always known. I had waited at the window for them, not her. I'd lifted my head from my work, my heart hammering, hoping I'd heard hoofbeats, hoping the crunch of leaves in the forest was one of them.

Guilt flooded through me at the realization.

"Do you want me to ask how long you're staying?" I asked.

"Oh, darling, don't be so sensitive," she said with a wave of her hand. "I'm only joking. I don't know how long I'm staying. The wolf prince is being stubborn, my dear. He's quite set on marrying that little usurper your father dragged back here. But don't worry, my dear, I'm working on them both."

"What's a usurper?" I asked, turning the word over. I liked the way it sounded, kind of slippery and hungry, the way my body felt when the boys were touching me.

"Don't worry your silly little head about it now," Mother Dear said with another wave of her hand.

"But I want to know," I said. "Is it a kind of animal?"

"No, silly," Mother Dear said, covering her heart and laughing like it was the funniest thing she'd ever heard. It used to make me feel strange when she did that, and now I knew why. She was laughing at my stupidity, except maybe I wasn't stupid. Maybe I'd just never learned that because I was too busy learning how to sing and dance and paint and sew and bake for my future as queen.

"Shouldn't I know these things if I'm going to be queen?" I asked. "If it's going to affect me, if it's keeping me from the prince, why can't I know?"

"Well," she said, her eyes widening and her laughter dying. "Aren't we uppity today?"

"I just want the truth, Mother," I said. "I don't see why that's so wrong."

"Astrid wants the truth now," Mother Dear said. "She's too good to sit around in a lovely tower swimming in treasure with not a care in the world. She's too good for the fine gowns I've bought her and the fancy dancing I've taught her. She's too good to spend time with her dear mother who slaves night and day to bring her a bright and shining future full of hope."

"I don't want a future full of hope," I said, throwing my hands up. "I want right now, full of whatever it holds, whether it's hope or pain or uncertainty. I want today. I want the past sixteen years of my life back."

As I spoke, my voice rose, and Mother Dear's pretty blue eyes got bigger and bigger. Then they snapped into narrow slits, and she strained forward as if she was barely holding herself back from leaping onto me and throttling me. "Of course," she said. "It's all about you. You don't care about me. You don't care that I'm doing this for your sake. I'm protecting you from the heartbreak and devastation that I endured by making sure that you never have to face that. I'm making up for all the things I didn't get to do in my life by making sure that you get the very best life. I'm sorry that it's taken me so long, Astrid. I'm not perfect. I don't get a happy ending. But you can, if you'll just have a little more patience."

"I don't care about a happy ending," I said. "And who's to say your happy ending would be happy for me? I want my life to be my own. I don't want to sit up here sewing and wallowing in my own tears. I want to be down there with everyone else."

Mother Dear's eyes flashed with that unearthly fire that she had instead of treasure, and I knew I'd said the wrong thing. "Everyone else?" she asked, her lips pulled back in a grin even as she spoke through clenched teeth. "Who is everyone else, Astrid? Has that boy been back to visit you? Is that it? While I'm out there trying to secure your marriage, you're back here spreading your legs for any Romeo who calls up to your window, ruining yourself for your husband? It's one thing to marry a stupid princess, quite another to marry a stupid slut."

I shook my head, backing away as I saw the veins pulsing in her neck. Though I didn't know all the words she used, tears filled my eyes at the venom in her voice. "What if I don't want to marry the wolf prince?" I asked. "Can't I marry a shifter prince?"

"There is no shifter prince," she snarled. "And if there were, he would be your brother. Though knowing what you came from, I wouldn't expect that to stop you."

"What does that mean?" I asked. "Where did I come from?"

"Do you really think a strong woman like me could produce a sniveling weakling like you?" she asked. "Even you can't be that stupid."

"What do you mean?" I asked again, swiping the tears from my cheek before they could solidify.

"If you had a boy up here, you've turned out to be trash despite my best efforts," she said, striding to the window. "I'll have shutters made so that you can't see them again, and no one can get in."

Despite my promise to myself, a cry burst from my lips. "No," I said, running to the window and grasping her hands in desperation.

"You have been seeing that boy," she cried, her face triumphant. "I knew it. But don't worry, my dear. I won't let anything bad happen to you, my princess. I'll protect you from the harlot's tragic fate."

"Don't close the windows," I begged. "It's all I have. You can't lock me in the dark."

"Oh, but you had to have a taste of love, didn't you? Foolish girl. All men will tell you lies to get what they want from you. They don't love you. Only I love you."

"They do," I whispered.

"You're as crazy as your father's first wife if you think love alone will be enough. It won't, Astrid. You'll grow old, and the men won't line up for a turn with you then. They'll turn their back on you for the hand of a woman who is richer, prettier, younger. All the singing in the world can't save a bird when it's in the cat's mouth. The teeth of time will chew you up and leave nothing but feathers."

"Then let me go down there before that happens," I said. "Let me out."

"Oh, darling, I wish I could," she said. "I wanted to give you a good life, to keep you from those people your father rules, shifters who dwell in their own filth, poverty and shame. You're not equipped to handle that life. You're fragile."

"I'm not," I insisted.

"Life out there is hard. It would break you, Astrid."

I could've told her the hard truth in return for hers—that it was no better to be broken by her than life. At least that way I would've lived.

Instead, I lowered my head and nodded, pretending to wipe at tears. I needed her to leave, even if it meant she was going to get wood to board up the windows. I couldn't let her find Daniel, not with how angry she was.

"I was going to stay and have a nice dinner with you, but you've ruined my good mood," she said. "Lower me down. I'll be back tomorrow. I hope you can spend this time being properly ashamed of yourself for what you've done with that boy. In the meantime, I'll be chopping that vine on the way down."

She climbed into the basket, ordering me to lower her slowly. Halfway down, she brought out a long knife from her skirts and began to hack at the vines, tearing them away from the wall. Tears gathered in my eyes as I watched her bruise and tatter the lush green leaves, shredding the vines that had brought life to my window at last.

When she had finished, she ordered me to lower her to the ground. An overwhelming urge to drop her trembled through me, and my fingers clenched on the rope. I could let go. I could drop her so easily.

But she wouldn't die. She was invincible. She would fly out of her body and come up here and steal mine, a body that was even younger than hers. Then she could live the life she always wanted with my body and her brain. She'd be the

127

princess, rich with treasure and a voice like a siren, but she wouldn't be the talentless idiot she raised. She would still be herself inside.

I shivered at the thought. I knew she couldn't push me out of my body—yet. She had practiced on me, growing stronger as I resisted, but she couldn't push me out. If she did, I would die. She'd told me that she'd never push hard enough to kill me. But now I wasn't sure. Maybe it was only a matter of time. Once she grew strong enough to push me out, she might not hold back. She might just take my body. I had to get out before then.

Without releasing the rope, I lowered her the rest of the way. No matter how tempting, no matter how angry I became, I could never kill someone.

Mother Dear stepped out of the hair basket, then reached up as high as she could, and with a swipe of her knife, severed the rope.

"There," she called. "Now if your lover comes calling, you won't be tempted to lift him up."

I didn't answer, though I had to press my lips together to keep from yelling after her that it was too late, he was already up here in this very room with me. In fact, she had left us trapped in the room together, and if we continued where we'd left off, he'd show me even more pleasures she didn't want me to know about. She wanted me to live the life she'd never had, but not experience anything good of my choosing.

I was done with that, though. I was ready to choose.

Chapter Sixteen

Daniel

I sat in the dark for what felt like hours, trying to make sense of what was around me. I couldn't see. The room was as black as the back of a blind man's eyelid. But once I reached the bottom of the ladder, I'd tried to feel my way across the room. I hadn't gotten far before I slipped on something loose on the floor. I almost fell, but at the last second, my hand caught the ladder. I stood there, my heart pounding and my breath coming fast.

I didn't know exactly what the witch would do if she caught me. I hated thinking what she might be doing to Astrid up there. But I figured Astrid knew how to handle her mother by now. She'd hidden me down here, so her mother wouldn't know, and I wasn't about to screw it all up by falling on my clumsy ass. I slid my foot along the floor, feeling the shifting surface. Then I lowered myself, not daring to walk and risk making noise. I'd heard horror stories about witches—everyone had. Witches ate babies, or they'd curse your future children if you so much as bumped into them in a store and didn't apologize.

I knew Astrid wasn't like that, but her mom? No guarantees. I'd seen her around the Third Valley a few times. Besides the doctor, who served all supernatural creatures in the Three Valleys, she was the only witch I'd ever seen in our valley. People said she'd put a spell on the king, made him fall in love with her. Recently I'd heard that she was a body snatcher who was on probation from the coven for snatching another witch's body. I didn't pay much attention to gossip about witches since it had never concerned me. Until now.

I strained to make out the words above as Astrid and her mother talked, but I couldn't. At the same time, my hands groped along the floor. It felt like I was sitting in a pile of smooth, cold pebbles. I picked one up and held it between two fingers, tracing its shape. It was rounded on one end, pointed on the other, and as smooth as if it had been shaped in a mold.

It seemed familiar somehow, but I wasn't sure how. I dropped it and picked up a handful more. They were cold as they dribbled through my fingers. I plucked out one and then another, examining them in the dark. Slightly heavy and cold and smooth as metal, each one shaped like a single teardrop.

I crawled around a bit, never finding a wall. The room felt enormous, cavernous. My stomach lurched when I imagined an opening just in front of me, invisible in the darkness. I stopped crawling and sat down to wait. The ladder hadn't been very tall, and if there was a hole that dropped down to the bottom of the lighthouse, I'd be nothing but a splatter on the ground when Astrid came to get me.

At long, long last, she did. The trapdoor opened, and I jumped up, ready to ask one of the million questions I had. But my voice died when her bare foot and slender ankle appeared. What if her mother had forced her to give me up, and she'd come down with her?

"She's gone," Astrid said, as if sensing my unease. "It's safe."

"What is this place?" I asked, looking around as the light from above filtered down. When she'd pushed me down through the door, I'd barely had time to grab the ladder. It had looked pitch dark after the light above, and I hadn't seen anything. Now, as the light filtered down, I could see piles and piles of sparkling…gold.

My eyes must have been bugging out of my head, but Astrid just smiled kind of shy. "It's my treasure."

"Fuck me," I said. "When you said treasure, you actually meant treasure."

"Yeah," she said, hooking an arm through the rungs of the ladder and perching about halfway down.

"Man. When Jack stole those beans, he was hoping for a couple diamonds. This is probably worth more than a thousand diamonds. You're literally sitting on a gold mine."

"Yeah," she said again, looking adequately guilty about that.

"Where did you get it?" I asked, looking around, trying to comprehend. It was weird enough that a lighthouse was here, but now I'd found an entire pirate ship's worth of treasure inside it.

"I cried it out."

I gaped at her, my mouth hanging open. No wonder her mother kept her locked up here. She wasn't just the princess. She was a freaking golden goose.

But then I saw her looking back at me, a strange little smile on her face. I hadn't grown up with three brothers to become a complete sucker.

"You didn't cry this out," I said. "People don't cry out treasure. Not even witches."

"You can make me cry if you don't believe me."

"I can't make you cry."

"It's not that hard," she said, gesturing around the room. "I've cried lots in my life."

My stomach turned raw and sour at the thought of her crying even a handful of tears, let alone a whole room full. "Your mother made you cry all these tears?"

"Not all of them," she said. "Sometimes I cried because I wanted to see Father Dear, or just because I was lonely."

"So, your mother made you cry all these tears."

She shrugged. "I used to be afraid of the dark. She'd lock me down here to make me cry until I had no more tears."

I swallowed, trying to imagine being locked down here, never knowing what was in the dark with me. The terror of that little girl she had been gnawed at me like some evil monster lurking in the shadows.

"We have to get you out of here," I said. "Now."

She hesitated, chewing at her luscious lips. "Can you keep this a secret?"

"This?" I asked, gesturing around to the mountains of tears. They didn't seem precious now that I knew where they'd come from. Astrid's pain was too high a price to pay even for red gold tears.

She nodded. "I don't want your brothers to think... I just don't want them to see me as..."

"A commodity?"

"I trust them," she said. "Mother Dear always said people would use me for my tears, and I don't think you would or that your brothers would, but..."

"They wouldn't."

"I don't want to put them in danger," she said. "Even knowing about this could put you in danger. I would have hidden you somewhere else if I'd known she would leave so soon. I would have hidden you under the bed."

"That's what I found on the floor," I said.

She nodded, then gripped the ladder and stood. "I'm ready."

A minute later, we stood at the window looking out at the rising moon. I couldn't resist sliding an arm around her middle, pulling her back against me. I pressed my nose into her hair, remembering the way she smelled, the way she tasted. A throb of desire shot through me, but I refocused my attention. First and foremost, I needed to get her out of this place.

"You think you can fly down?" I asked.

"Mother Dear took the basket," she said. "But I'll make a loop at the end. You can put your foot in it and hold onto the rope while I lower you. You'll have to jump the last few feet."

"I'm not worried about me," I said. "How are you getting down?"

She held her head high and threw back her shoulders. "I'm a bird," she said. "I'm going to fly."

Chapter Seventeen

Jack

When Evan and I got home from work, we found only William in the house. Mom was at work, but Daniel should have been around.

"He snuck off to see Astrid," William said with a grin. I won't lie, jealousy flared up inside me like a dragon about to spew fire all over the place. It wasn't like Astrid was mine. I hadn't even found her first. But some part of me didn't care about the logic. It thought of her as mine. At least, I wanted her to be. William wasn't the only one who couldn't shut up about her.

Actually, I could shut up about her, but I couldn't shut off my mind. It was always on her like some kind of lovesick puppy. Every day I had to talk myself out of running up there just to sit outside her window and hear her singing. I didn't know what had happened between her and Evan—despite appearances, he was too much a gentleman to kiss and tell. But I'd caught him staring off into space a few times, even smiling to himself as he worked. That was very un-Evan-like behavior. And I was pretty damn sure I knew the cause.

To be fair, Daniel was the only one who hadn't gotten a chance to hang out with her alone yet, so I couldn't fault the guy. But every time one of my brothers got to spend time with her, I wished it had been me. Not that I blamed them or begrudged them. I just wished I could have been there, too. I would have been happy just to sit in the corner like I wasn't even there as long as I could watch Astrid. The way she moved, like grace itself. The way she talked with her whole body, her hands, her face, always moving. The way she could stand before us without a stitch on her glorious body and not show a trace of shame or modesty. It was intoxicating. She was intoxicating.

"When did Daniel go up there?" I asked, nodding at the darkening window.

William frowned and drew his shoulders up toward his ears. "This morning."

I shot Evan a look, and he raised his eyebrows. "Told you not to mess with a witch."

"Shit," I said, peeling off my shirt. "We'd better go find him."

"Now?" William asked. "It's almost dark."

"We're sure as hell not waiting for morning," I said. "The gods only know what she's done to him if she caught him."

A few minutes later, the three of us took off along the road, cutting away from it and heading up the mountain until we reached the clearing around the tower. We shifted back into human form to talk.

"How do we know if he's in there?" William asked. "What if she caught him on the way in?"

"He's in there," I said. "I could smell him before I shifted."

"Is she in there?" he asked, peering anxiously at the tower. The vines climbing up it had been butchered, and a dark shape lay crumpled on the ground below it. My chest tightened at the sight of it, but when I crept forward, I could see that it wasn't big enough to be a human.

"Is it her?" William hissed.

"No," I said, creeping closer still. It wasn't her, but it had once been a part of her. When I picked it up, I recognized her basket, now shredded beyond repair. All the work she must have done to make it, destroyed.

Something glinted in the dirt, and when I bent, I saw a tiny teardrop-shaped gem sparkling in the light of the rising moon. I had more important things to worry about than earrings, though, and I didn't have a pocket to keep it, so I left it where it lay.

"Astrid," I called. "Can you hear us?"

A moment later, her face appeared in the window. "Jack?" she asked.

"Yes," I said, so much relief flooding through me that I thought I'd faint dead away like a girl in a dramatic black-and-white movie. But goddamn, it was good to see her face. For a second, I just gazed at her, forgetting what else to say. I was so fucked. If she told me she was in love with one of my brothers, I thought I'd have to move in with our deadbeat dad just so I wouldn't have to see them together all the time and know I couldn't have her.

"You came to visit me?" Astrid asked, like she couldn't believe I'd do that just for her. Crazy, because I'd do a lot more than walk up a mountain to see her. I would have moved the entire mountain with a teaspoon if it meant I could look up and see her smiling down at me like that.

Evan cleared his throat from the darkness behind me, and I shook myself out of my crazy love haze. "Evan and William came, too," I said. "Is Daniel with you?"

"I'm about to lower him down."

"Is he okay? Can you lift me up without your basket?"

"No," she said.

"We can't come up?" I asked, my chest caving in with disappointment. I'd been so excited to see her.

"No," she said. "I'm coming down."

Chapter Eighteen

Astrid

I lowered Daniel in the makeshift harness we'd made from the rope. He had to jump the last eight feet or so, but he assured me he was fine. And then it was my turn. My turn to leave the tower.

I stared down, the drop suddenly seeming like a hundred times a hundred feet. I'd been so determined just minutes before, but now I hesitated. Could I do it? What if Mother Dear had been telling the truth all that time, and the world out there was cold and cruel, and people caught me and used me and wouldn't let me go? What if she'd been right about me? What if I was too weak and stupid to make it outside my tower?

But then I looked down, and four boys were standing beneath my window looking up at me, waiting for me. Daniel, who was so happy and had made me so happy today, was grinning and dusting off his clothes after the fall. Evan looked like he didn't really care one way or another what I did, but he didn't look away, either. He was waiting to see if I had the guts. William stood beside him with hands clasped together in front of his chest as if he couldn't wait for this moment. And Jack was there, gazing up at me with so much emotion it almost scared me back into my room to hide away again.

What if I didn't live up to his expectation? What if he thought I was the sort of princess Mother Dear had tried to make me?

I pushed away that thought. Despite the purple and gold gown I'd chosen to wear for my escape, the boys all knew I was just me underneath it. With that thought in mind, I ducked back into the room and peeled it off, wrapping it carefully before tossing it down. I was ready. I was tired of letting Mother Dear make all the plans while I waited for something to happen, for life to begin. Tonight, I had my own plans. Tonight, I would make something happen. Tonight, I would live.

My heart stampeded in my chest, nervousness and giddiness mixing to make me nearly dizzy.

I stepped up to the open window, pleased when I heard a few of the boys suck in a breath when they saw me standing there wearing nothing but the moonlight. I eased myself out and slowly stood, my toes gripping the sill, my back pressed to the wall above the window. I flattened my hands against the rough white paint on the lighthouse wall, closed my eyes, and took a deep breath.

"Shift first," Jack said. "I can come up and fly down with you if you want."

I shook my head, my toes clenched, holding on for dear life. I wanted to go. I just had to do it. But something inside me balked, refusing to take the last step.

Daniel cupped his hands around his mouth and yelled up to me. "Come on, Astrid. Show them what you showed me."

Pride swelled inside me again. I'd impressed him with how well I could fly. Now I wanted to impress the others. I motioned for them to step back, and they retreated to the edge of the trees.

"You don't have to jump if you don't want to," William said. "I'll come up and lower you down."

"Just jump," Evan called. "You can do it."

I could do it. I'd been waiting for this moment all my life. Why was I even hesitating?

"Goodbye, home," I whispered. I spread my fingers and toes, releasing my hold on my old life. My body tipped forward, plummeting toward the ground. I heard one of the boys shout in alarm, but I had already thrown out my arms, ready to fly. Suddenly, a horrible thought ripped through my mind. What if Mother Dear had put a spell on me to keep me from shifting outside the tower? The ground rushed at me faster than I had imagined it could. The prickling tingle of feathers swept over my arms, and I almost cried out in relief. But the ground was coming up so fast.

I beat my arms at the air, grasping for friction. I could see the pebbles under my window, the glint of the moonlight off something shiny. And then my wings caught the air, and I was buoyed up, flapping hard as I soared across the clearing.

I smacked into Jack's chest at full speed. He caught me, laughing and cursing at the same time.

"That was so badass," Daniel said, ruffling my feathers.

Jack stroked his hand along my back, cradling my body in the crook of his arm.

"You're crazy," William said, bending down to tickle the bottom of my clawed feet. "I can't believe you did that."

"That was really fucking stupid," Jack said, but he was laughing. He sounded a little choked, too, and he squeezed my body against him like he'd thought he'd never get to do it again.

Was I crazy, like Mother Dear had said? Was I stupid to have done that, and I wouldn't last a day in the real world? My heart was beating so hard in my falcon chest that I thought I might die of a heart attack before I made it out of the clearing.

When I'd calmed down, I shifted back into my human form. I hadn't considered the logistics of that move, and I ended up standing in the crook of Jack's arm, my body halfway in front of his. He held onto me another second, his arm around my middle and his face pressed into my neck. "Don't ever do that again," he murmured.

The heat of his body raged up my back like a flame, and a shiver washed over my front side, the one not pressed against him. I closed my eyes and leaned back against Jack, letting my head fall against his shoulder. He buried his nose to my hair, inhaling deeply before releasing me.

Daniel handed me the bundle I'd tossed down, a crooked grin on his face. "You'll need this before you reach civilization."

That's when it hit me. I was standing on the ground. Gritty dirt and pebbles were under my feet instead of smooth boards. I dug my toes into the ground. "I—I'm out," I said.

"Yep," Jack said, giving me a gentle push forward. "You're free."

"I'm free," I repeated, stepping further from the boys. My steps were hesitant at first, as if the ground might snap me up and swallow me whole. I just couldn't believe I was out of my tower. Walking around on the ground. I ran forward into the grass, then stopped, gasping in shock. It was cold and slightly damp, almost vibrating with lifeforce. I buried my toes in it, clinging to it the way I'd clung to the ledge. I was never leaving the ground again, not ever.

I felt a flutter inside me like wings beating in protest. Oh, yeah. I had a bird nature, too, and it wasn't a grouse or a penguin. She obviously needed to leave the ground.

"What do I do?" I asked, turning back toward the boys.

They met my question with blank stares.

"I don't know what to do with myself," I said. "I'm free. It's so big."

"There's a whole world waiting for you to explore," Jack said, his warm smile shining in the moonlight like all the treasure in the world.

"It's yours for the taking," Daniel said, throwing out his arms.

"It's just so much," I said, wrapping my arms around myself. I felt like the sky was so high it was going to fly off into space, and the earth was so big I might come loose and go tumbling down it and never stop. I had always lived in my one room. If I needed a change, I could go downstairs to the treasure room for a while. My life, my world, was the size of two large rooms.

And now it wasn't. Now it had no boundaries, no size. It was endless. I felt so small, like a speck of dust in the big world. Even the clearing was too big, too open. The trees might come crashing down at any moment. The earth would stretch on and on in every direction, and I wouldn't know where to go or when to stop.

"It's okay," Jack said, his warm hand coming to rest on my back.

I was breathing so hard that black spots had started to take over my vision.

"I should go back," I blurted.

"Just breathe," William said, coming up on my other side and laying a hand in the middle of my back. "Rest your hands on your knees and breathe through it."

"You got this," Daniel said, reaching in to place his hand on my side.

Without a word, Evan laid a hand between my shoulder blades. Their touch anchored me, so I didn't feel like I'd float up to the stars without anything holding me back.

There was nothing holding me back.

I straightened, staring at one of them and then the next. "There's nothing holding me back."

Jack nodded, his face guarded and wary.

William blinked at me from behind his glasses, all concern.

"There's nothing holding me back," I repeated.

Evan nodded, a little smile tugging at the corner of his mouth.

"You know it, baby," Daniel said, grabbing me and picking me up, spinning me around as he had before.

"I can go anywhere," I said. "I can do anything."

"First get dressed," Evan said, handing me the bundle I'd dropped when I started to unravel.

I unwrapped the dress, a fine purple gown that I'd made by hand. It was heavy, with threads made of real gold and strips of purple velvet in between wider panels of hand-sewn brocade.

"That's an interesting choice for hiking," Jack said.

"Should I wait to put it on?" I asked, hesitating halfway into the thing. "I could go without clothes like all of you."

"Naked hiking isn't the best experience, either," Daniel said. "Y'all should shift. I'll ride the horse since I have clothes. If you get tired of flying, Astrid, you can ride with me."

"So unfair," William grumbled to Evan. "You get to have a hot girl riding you, and I get to be a cow."

"I get to have Daniel riding my ass," Evan said.

We all shifted and started off down the mountain. I usually shifted into a falcon, but I'd tried out almost every kind of bird I could think of when I'd been learning to fly. Now, I shifted into an owl, so I could see in the dark. The moon had risen higher, but it was too dark for most bird eyes.

"You're a really talented shifter," Daniel said as we started down the mountain. "Most people have trouble shifting into other forms."

I couldn't do more than hoot in answer, but in truth, I could only shift easily into various birds. I still shuddered at the memory of trying to force my body into the form of a turtle, and since learning I could shift into other animals, I'd tried to shift into a few things without much success.

Jack led the way down the mountain, followed by Daniel on horseback and William in bull form. I swooped overhead, resting frequently on branches. The more I flew, the easier it became to land. Maybe all I'd really needed was more space to practice. Out here I had enough space to curve my wings to catch the air and slow myself, then to grip onto a branch and settle while the land animals caught up again.

Soon enough, we were at the bottom of the mountain, and a wide dirt path cut through the forest. I'd seen roads from my tower, but none up close like this. I marveled at it while Daniel dismounted. The others shifted into human form, so I did, too, though I wouldn't have minded flying all night long. With the cool breeze ruffling my feathers and the bright moon overhead, I could have stayed out there forever.

Daniel handed my dress to me, and the others got out a bag they had stashed in a tree. We all dressed before starting down the road.

"Ready to meet our mom?" Jack asked, giving me a smile that seemed to hold more meaning than I could decipher.

"Sure," I said. A minute later, we turned into a driveway where a home of some sort sat. At least, I thought it was a home. It didn't look like the castles in the illustrated tales I'd read, or even like the humble cottages. It was a rectangular metal box that sat up on square, grey stones, and it had only a couple tiny windows. Inside, one pale light burned.

Daniel bounded ahead and opened the door, bowing with a flourish as he gestured for us to enter. Jack gave me a tight-lipped smile and held my hand to help me up the steps. My foot caught on the hem of my dress, and I lurched forward, almost tumbling on my face before I'd even made it in the door. I yanked at the fabric, finally jerking it out from under my toes.

"Once again, she knows how to make an entrance," Evan said as I stumbled into the trailer. A woman was inside, sitting on a long, puffy chair with cracked cushions, watching a group of tiny people inside a glass box. She had a worn, wrinkled face that wasn't nearly as beautiful as Mother Dear's, and she wore a pair of jeans and a plaid shirt instead of a dress. I reminded myself that she hadn't known I was coming.

"Mom, this is Astrid," Jack said, squaring his shoulders and resting a hand on my lower back.

"The princess," William added.

"Oh, look at you," the woman said, rising from the cushioned seat. She reached toward me, holding her hand sideways instead of palm up. I wasn't sure what to do. Mother Dear had taught me how to give my hand to a boy for a kiss, but not a woman. After a second, I laid my hand over the top of hers. She clasped my hand in both of hers and shook it up and down.

"It's nice to meet you, Astrid," she said. "You're…Owen's daughter?"

"Yes," I said, brightening at the familiar name of Father Dear. Everything here was so different that I didn't know what to do.

"Ah," she said, nodding. "That makes sense, then. That's why I haven't see you around the valley. Who's your mother, dear?"

"Mother Dear," I said. "Or, Yvonne. That's her first name."

She cast a questioning look at the boys, who did some shuffling and shrugging and cutting their eyes at each other. "The witch," Jack said at last.

"Oh!" their mom said, drawing back. "Yvonne the witch? That explains the fine clothes."

"It does?"

"Oh, well, you'd just never see that kind of thing in the Third Valley," she said. "You know what they say. Third Valley, third class." She gave a little laugh that sounded forced, gesturing to her clothes.

I didn't know what she meant, but then it dawned on me. She hadn't prepared a feast or dressed for the occasion because she wasn't a noble. She was a commoner who would come to see me when I paraded through town on coronation day.

"Are you...seeing Jack?" she asked, giving her son a questioning look.

"Something like that," Daniel said with a grin.

"Well, you're welcome to hang out here, if that's what you kids want. You can see we don't have a lot to do, but it's nice of the boys to finally bring home a girl for me to meet." She sat down on the couch again and put her feet on a funny, low table in front of her.

"It's not like that," Jack said, his face going a little pink.

"Like what?" I asked.

"I'll explain later," he said, his fingers brushing my lower back again. I sighed and leaned back into him, and he stumbled at little, like I'd caught him by surprise.

"Are those elves?" I said, nodding toward the glass box.

"No, those are people," Jack said, looking like he was trying not to laugh again. "That's a TV, Astrid. It's not real."

"How did they get in there?" I asked, leaning down to look closer. "Did you give them a shrinking brew?"

All four boys started laughing, and their mother stared at me. "You don't have TV in your valley?"

"No," I said. "What is it?"

"We can explain all that later," Evan said. "Let's figure out what we're going to do with you. Where are you going to stay?"

"I thought I could see the people," I said. "How they live and everything. If I'm going to rule them one day…"

"Didn't you tell her?" their mother said, frowning at the boys. "Astrid, honey. The shifter king, or queen in your case, doesn't really have any control over his people. He's not really a ruler. He's more of a…symbol."

"Not a very good one, either," Evan muttered.

"What do you mean?" I asked. "I'm the princess. When he's done being king, I'll be coronated and take his place. I'll be the shifter queen."

"You can try," William said. "But shifters don't really stand on all that ceremony."

"But…Mother Dear said…"

"If you want to see how shifters live, look around," their mom said. "This is pretty much it. I'd invite you to stay, but we only have one bedroom for all four of the boys. I sleep out here on the couch." She patted the cushions under her. It didn't look wide enough for even a skinny person to sleep comfortably, not to mention the condition of it left a lot to be desired.

"Then I'll sleep here, too," I said. "If I'm going to be the princess, I should know how the people live. I should live and work right beside them, not sit up in my tower like a dragon hoarding treasure." I shot Daniel a smile as I quoted his earlier words.

"It's okay," Jack said. "We'll take her to her dad's. We just wanted to bring her by to introduce her."

The boys headed for the door, and even though I still had a million questions, I followed them out. "We're going to see Father?" I asked as we stepped out into the darkness.

"That's what she thinks," Jack said with a grin.

Chapter Nineteen

Astrid

"Where are we going?" I asked as we congregated in the yard outside.

"In through our window," Jack said, nodding toward the end of the boxy house. "You can stay as long as you want, and then we'll take you to a safe place where no one will look for you. Unless you want to go to your dad's."

"No," I said with a shiver. "My mother might be there."

"And we're here," Daniel said, wiggling his eyebrows at me.

"Exactly," I said. "Usually I just imagine you're there when I'm going to sleep. Tonight, you'll really be here."

"You think about us when you're going to sleep?" William asked as we headed for a small window. Jack popped out the screen and pushed open a glass window.

"Every night," I said. "I don't have much else to think about."

"Wow," Daniel said, hesitating at the window. "You just say whatever's on your mind, don't you?"

"Yes," I said. "Why wouldn't I?"

"Most girls... You know. They play hard to get."

"Is that good or bad?"

"You're good," Evan said, his voice a low rumble that made the hairs on the back of my neck stand up. He stepped up behind me, his hands settling on my hips. "Ready?"

"Do you think about me?" I asked.

"All the time," Jack said.

"Me, too," William said.

"Y'all are hopeless," Daniel said.

Evan snorted.

"Tell me you don't," Jack said.

"Never," Evan said, lifting me up to the window. I slid my arms through, then my head, then wormed my way in. It wasn't a tight fit, but it wasn't a big window like mine. I didn't know how the guys could fit through, but one at a time, they did.

"Welcome to our room," Daniel said, gesturing grandly to the tiny space. Two beds filled almost the entire room, with just a walkway between them and a small dresser at the end of each.

"Can I stay here tonight?" I asked. "All night?"

"We should really get you somewhere safer," Jack said. "This place isn't very good protection."

"Mother Dear probably won't be home tonight," I said. "She usually stays gone for days."

"What if she comes home?" Daniel asked.

"She won't know where I went," I said. "I'll go tomorrow. I promise. I just…everything is so new. I thought maybe I could be with someone familiar tonight."

"It's not that we don't want you to stay," Evan said.

"Really?" I asked. "You want me to stay?"

"More than anything," Jack said.

"Then it's settled," Daniel said.

"Since me and Jack are the ones thinking about you, you'll probably want to sleep in our bed," William said to me, gesturing at a bed.

"Hey," Daniel said. "That's not fair."

"You had your turn today," Evan said quietly.

"The lady can choose for herself," Jack said, his eyes fixed on me. They were serious for once, and more than that. They seemed to communicate with me, as if we shared an understanding. I could see how deeply he needed me, maybe even more than I needed him. My need was spread between all four of them, but Jack needed only me. I could read all this in his eyes, just the way I read my books. And somehow, I knew that he understood it all, too.

I tore my eyes from his, meeting William's next. He looked so full of hope, openly vulnerable to what I would choose. Daniel smiled, but he also looked bit resigned. His brother had spoken, and he respected his word. And Evan. Oh, Evan. The quiet one, who so rarely spoke when his brothers were there to do it for him, but who had spoken easily to me when we were alone. Evan, who had touched me in the rain, who had woken my body to this new desire that I'd never known before. He pressed his lips together and gave the slightest nod.

"What now?" William asked, looking around at his brothers.

"I should take a shower if I'm going to be sleeping next to Astrid," Jack said. "A cold one."

The guys gave each other looks that I didn't understand.

"I don't think it's supposed to rain," I said. "Cold or otherwise."

They blinked at me for a second. "Not a rain shower," William said. "A shower's how you get clean. Like a bath."

"Oh," I said. "Then why do you call it a shower?"

"It showers down on you," William said. "Come on, I'll show you."

"You can't take her out there," Daniel said. "Mom will see."

"I'll be a bird," I said. "I can ride on his shoulder, and she won't see me."

"Now that sounds more like a sixteen-year-old girl," Jack said with an approving grin.

I shifted and fluttered out of my gown, which Daniel picked up and laid across the bed. William took me in his hands and carried me out of the room, a few steps down a narrow passage, and into another room, this one even tinier than theirs. I'd never seen rooms so small.

I shifted back to human, which made William gulp. His face went pink, and he turned away to pull back a plasticky curtain.

"This is the shower," he said, gesturing at a small white tub. He turned a couple metal handles at one end, and rain rushed out of a metal spout above.

"Oh, wow," I said, laughing and clapping my hands together.

"It's warm, too," he said, smiling at my reaction. "Feel."

He stuck his hand out to catch the raindrops, and I did the same. It was warm—warmer than the warmest rain I'd ever felt. As warm as a bath. I searched the flat, dry wall where the water spout appeared and produced warm rain from nothing. "Is it magic?" I asked.

"Technology," he said. "So, yeah, I guess it's a sort of magic."

We stood there smiling at each other for a moment, letting warm rain pelt down on our hands. "Can I bathe in it?"

William's throat did that funny thing where the bump bobbed up and down. "Yeah."

I stepped in, holding back a little shriek of delight at the pleasure of having warm water beating down on me. It really was like a bath, and I loved baths. Now, I didn't even have to heat the water on the stove one kettle at a time and carry it to the tub. I just stepped in, and it ran over me. "You have to feel this," I said, reaching for William.

"Uh… Are you sure?" he stammered, his face going even more red.

"Yes, it feels amazing."

He looked at me a long moment. "I really can't leave, or Mom will see me leaving and hear the shower still running," he said at last. "But I could just…sit here while you shower?"

"You don't want to get in?"

"I do, but… Astrid. We'll be naked together."

"I know," I said, remembering what I'd done with Evan in the rain. "That feels good, too."

"You've been naked with a boy before?"

"Of course," I said. "I was naked with all of you."

"Yeah, but…not when you were alone with us."

"I was with Evan."

"Oh," he said, his face crumpling. "Well, see, that usually means that you like someone. And if you like Evan, then I probably shouldn't shower with you."

"But I like you, too," I said. "And it'll feel good for you, too. He told me."

"Are you sure?" William asked. "If he thinks you're his girlfriend or something…"

"I'm everyone's friend," I said. "And everyone should feel good. Daniel made me feel good today."

"Did he?" William asked, a funny look on his face. "How'd he do that?"

"He kissed me all over," I said. "I feel good with all of you, but especially when we're naked."

William hesitated, then peeled off his T-shirt. His skin was pale like mine instead of tan like Jack's, but he had the same freckles as Evan on his shoulders. He quickly dropped his shorts and stepped into the shower. I pulled him closer, so our bodies were pressed together the way that felt the best.

"I don't know how I feel about this," William said quietly, stroking my hair back.

"Doesn't it feel good?"

He swallowed, nodding.

"Then what's wrong with it?"

"Nothing," he said. "It's just…I'm not used to people being so…rational about it."

"I like to feel good," I said, turning to let the warmth splash over the front side of me.

"Let me wash your back," William said. He picked up the soap, running the bar over my skin. My body sighed with pleasure as his fingers kneaded my muscles, rubbing in the bubbles even as the warm water trickled over my shoulders. After a while, he put the soap back and kept massaging, rubbing my muscles, his fingers sliding over my slippery skin.

I leaned back against him with a sigh, warm and relaxed all the way through.

"Thank you," I said.

"Thank you for letting me serve you, princess," he said, a smile in his voice. He reached for the soap, lathering his hands before sliding them up the front of my body. "This is definitely payment in itself."

"Really?" I asked, arching into his touch.

"Yeah," he said, his voice incredulous. "This is…awesome."

"I told you it felt good."

"Okay," he said. "Let's make the most of it. I'm going to wash your feet like a real servant and work my way up from there."

By the time he finished, the water didn't feel as warm anymore, and I had turned to lava. I was so hot I thought my skin would start smoking at any moment, and so relaxed that my whole body felt limp. William had washed and massaged from my feet to my scalp, even shampooing my impossible hair.

"I think if I tried to fly right now, I'd flop on the ground like a jellyfish," I said. "My bones have melted."

"Me, too," William said, which I didn't understand, because I hadn't massaged him at all.

"Not all of you has melted," I said, pointing to the fifth limb that boys had.

"You can make it melt if you want," William said. "Trust me, it won't take long right now."

"Can I touch it?" I asked.

"You really don't have to ask," he said. "I just touched literally every inch of your body that's humanly possible to reach."

He was right about being relaxed. After only a few minutes, he pulled my hand away from massaging him, pressed out bodies together, and squeezed me hard until his muscles were shaking. Warmth bloomed between us, and William let out a low groan. After a long minute, he pulled away. "Sorry," he said, his face bright red as he pulled me under the water.

"Why?" I asked.

"Nothing," he muttered. He quickly lathered his hands and washed both our bellies, then turned off the water, which had gone tepid. After drying off, I shifted into a bird, and he wrapped a towel around himself before stepping into the hall.

"William?" his mom called from the room where she said. "I didn't hear you come in."

"Uh…maybe you dozed off."

"Who were you talking to in the shower? Did you bring that girl back here?"

"No, Mom," he said. "Leave me alone."

"I thought I heard a girl's voice."

"Do you see a girl?" William asked, gesturing back toward the bathroom, careful not to turn so she could see the bird on his other shoulder.

His mom sighed. "Goodnight, honey."

"Goodnight," William said, starting toward the bedroom.

"Oh, and William?"

He sighed. "Yeah?"

"I'm glad y'all have stopped drinking. If the girl's the reason for that, you can tell your brother that she's welcome here any time, witch or no."

Chapter Twenty

Astrid

"Good shower?" Evan asked, cocking an eyebrow and smirking at us.

"So, that's how it's going to be," Daniel said with a huge grin. "When you said show her the shower, you didn't mean show her how to work it and leave like a gentleman. And I thought I was the dog."

"You gotta grab the bull by the horns, right?" Jack asked with a wink.

"Did you hear Mom?" William asked. "She said Astrid is welcome here any time. I guess that means we're all good tonight."

"Since when do you care about breaking Mom's rules?" Daniel asked.

William shrugged and set me down on the bed. "I want her to like Astrid, that's all."

"I bet you do," Daniel said.

I shifted back into human form, and they all gaped at me for a second. I was starting to appreciate the power of being naked.

Jack hopped up from the bed and rifled through the dresser. While we showered, he'd changed into a pair of drawstring pants that hung low on his hips, and I took a moment to admire him as he searched the drawers. It wasn't just my naked body that had power. It was everyone's. I thought of how good it felt to be pressed up against William with the warm water flowing over us and nothing between us. How firm and wide Evan's chest was. The strength in Daniel's ropey arms. And the lines on Jack's lower abdomen that formed a V-shape pointing down into his pants that made me gulp.

He turned and handed me a folded T-shirt and a pair of shorts. "We wanted to talk to you," he said. "Now that you're back from your couple shower."

"Okay," I said, pulling the shirt over my head. It smelled like soap and a faint hint of Jack.

Jack sat down beside me. "We were just talking about how this is going to work."

"You mean hiding from your mom tonight?"

"No," he said, running his palms down the front of his thighs. "With us."

I turned to the others for help, but they were all looking at me expectantly, as if waiting for an answer. "I'm sorry," I said, shaking my head. "What's the question again?"

"I know you've been busy, you know, running away from home and worrying about where to live so you probably haven't thought about it, but…well, we have."

I nodded, though I still didn't know what he was asking. I waited for him to go on.

"We don't have to talk about it now if you don't want, but we just wanted you to know that we all like you."

"I like all of you, too."

"We don't want to pressure you into anything," Jack said. "So, you can have the bed and a couple of us can sleep on the floor. Or, if you want one of us to sleep in the bed, the other one will sleep on the floor. And you don't have to do anything but sleep. We're not expecting anything."

"Whoever you want to be with, we're going to say yes, though," Daniel said, his grin in place. He wiggled his eyebrows, giving me a meaningful look. "You already got a taste of what I have to offer."

My body tingled at the memory of his mouth on my skin.

"We all know you've been…doing stuff…with my brothers, and we're totally okay with that," Jack said. "I just wanted you to know that we talked, and it's not a secret. So, you don't have to feel strange about being open with us, or like you have to sneak around the way we are with Mom."

"I don't," I said.

"And if you want to do more, we're okay that you're exploring your sexuality with us," Jack said. "In fact, it's pretty awesome. We're not going to think anything about it if you want to…you know. Experiment until you figure out who you want to be with. It's not like we're pillars of purity, and you've never had a chance to do any of that, so you're curious about different people. And that's totally cool."

I nodded again.

"So…just let us know," he said. "You take the lead. You can do as much or little as you want. You can always tell us what you want, or when to stop, and we'll respect that, no questions asked. We want you to be comfortable and have fun and enjoy yourself. With whoever you want to be with."

"I want to be with all of you," I said.

"But, like, who do you want to be your boyfriend?" William asked.

"All of you."

They looked at each other. After a minute, Evan shrugged. "Works for me."

"Witches do have more than one guy," Daniel said. "I never thought I'd want to be one of those guys, but…"

"But we'd never met you," Jack said, his knuckles brushing my knee. Warmth spread up my leg, settling between my thighs. I seemed to have an endless hunger there that woke at the touch of a hand.

"So…if you're ready for bed," Jack said. "Just tell us who you want in your bed."

"This is fine," I said. "Like we said earlier. I'll sleep between you and William."

Jack swallowed. "I might need that cold shower first."

"That's all there is left," William said with a smug smile. "We used all the hot water."

"Perfect," Jack said, standing and sauntering out of the room. Though he'd been the first boy I'd ever seen up close, the first boy I'd ever talked to, or smelled, or touched, I hadn't been as physically close to him. I wondered how his hands would feel on my skin, how warm his mouth would be, what he would feel like under his clothes. I longed to be as close to him as I'd been with the others, to feel as good with him as I had with them.

Instead, I slid into the bed beside William as Evan switched off the light. Jack hadn't asked me to shower with him, after all. I didn't know why, but I had this funny feeling like I'd done something wrong, but I didn't know what. Then William scooted over and kissed my cheek. "Thanks for the shower," he whispered. "This is officially the best night of my life."

And then I felt all better.

When Jack came back a few minutes later, the four of us were all in bed. Jack slid into bed carefully, as if afraid he might wake us, but I was still wide awake.

I scooted toward him, reaching out. He lay on his back, his hands at his sides, like Mother Dear always left her empty bodies. I snuggled close, as I had with the bodies, but I didn't have to pretend he was awake or fully alive. When I laid my hand over his heart, I could feel it pounding hard inside his chest instead of slow and faint like an animated corpse. His skin was cold and damp from the shower, but I could already feel the heat under it coiling up, rising to meet my palm.

Jack curled his arm around me, pulling me against him. "You're awake."

"I shouldn't be," I whispered in the darkness. "This was the longest day of my whole life."

The day played over in my mind, all the strangeness and wonder of it. Daniel climbing up and making my body feel alive. Mother Dear coming home and telling me I wasn't really her daughter. Leaving my tower for the very first time, and learning about a shower, the poverty of shifters, and that they didn't really care about princesses at all. From what his mother had said, she seemed more concerned with the fact that I was part witch.

"You can go to sleep," Jack said. "We'll keep you safe."

"Thank you." I ran my hand across the expanse of muscle in his chest, then down over the ridges in his abs. I circled a finger around his bellybutton, stroking the tiny hairs that grew there. His skin shivered, but he didn't move. "Do you want to touch me, too?" I whispered.

"Do you want me to?"

"Yes."

"My brothers are all right there."

"I know."

"You don't care?"

"I want them to be here," I said. "I like knowing we're all together."

"You're one of a kind," he said with a whisper-laugh. He rolled toward me, wrapping his arms around me.

"I know," I said. "That's because I'm the only real princess."

"No," he said. "It's because you're you. No more and no less."

No one had ever said anything like that to me. I had always been the princess, prepared to play a part, to gain an advantage. I was a bargaining chip, a maker of treasure, someone's daughter. I had never just been me. And I loved it.

I slid my hands over Jack's smooth, warm skin while my feet slid against his, tangling with them under the sheets.

"Can I kiss you?" he asked, cradling my cheek in his palm.

I remembered Daniel's mouth on my body, and I nodded. Instead of pushing off the blanket and moving down, he lifted my chin up. His mouth brushed mine, and a thousand stars shimmered to life inside me. No one had ever kissed me like that, so softly it was like he feared I'd crumble to dust and disappear if he pressed too hard. But I knew I wouldn't. I knew because the others had shown me. They may not have kissed my mouth, but they hadn't been afraid.

The others had all made me feel good, but they hadn't wanted me to do anything. Jack's mouth demanded a response. I pressed my lips harder against his, marveling at how much sensation was in my lips. His lips responded to mine, pressing harder, then softer again. His hand still cradled my face, his thumb stroking my cheek. Somehow, even having our mouths touching with all these clothes between us still made my heart pound and my blood sing.

I could feel every change in pressure, the heat of his mouth hidden inside. Slowly, his lips opened against mine, drawing mine open. He drew my lip gently between his teeth, his tongue tracing along it, then let my lip slide out again. I gasped at the warm wetness between his teeth, and a shudder of longing went through me. I hooked my leg over his hip, squirming against him to get that delicious feeling when his hardness pressed against my softness.

Jacks' tongue slid against mine, the friction of it making my whole body feel as wet as the inside of his mouth. I moved my tongue against his, tasting him, inhaling the scent of his skin. It was different, having something to do. It made me not only want to learn about my own body, which I'd never paid much attention to, but to learn all about his. I wanted to wake his blood the way Daniel had woken mine. I wanted to make him feel as good as he made me feel.

We kissed, and kissed, and kissed. Jack rolled onto his back, pulling me on top of him. I liked lying along the warm, hard length of his body, feeling our breath synchronize, our hearts beating together in mutual rhythm like a dance. I sat up to tug off my shirt, wanting my skin against his. Then I lay back down and kissed him more, until I was drowning in all the need coursing through me. The more I squirmed against him, the more I needed.

I remembered what Evan had said the first time I'd felt like this, when I'd told him to make it go away. He'd said that sex was like what we did, only bigger. Today everything I'd done had been big. "Do you want to do sex?" I whispered.

Jack hesitated, then drew back. "Right now?"

"Yes."

Jack's hands rested on my sides. "Are you sure? Now? We don't even know each other that well, and we're not alone…"

"Stop questioning it, or I'll come over there and do it for you," Daniel said, his voice muffled like he was speaking through a pillow.

"I want to feel good," I said.

"There are other ways," Jack whispered, his hands moving down to my waist, my hips.

"I've had other ways," I said. "Evan said it's even better than those. Is something wrong with sex? Why don't you want to try it?"

"I do," he said, his voice kind of choked. "There's nothing wrong with it. I just want you to be sure."

"I am sure," I said. "If it feels good, I don't see why you have to know each other well or be alone. I like you, and I want to feel good with you."

"It can hurt a little the first time."

"You're not going to talk her out of it," William said from across the bed. "She's very persistent."

"Let me get a condom," Jack said.

"Where is it?" I asked, running my fingers down the front of his neck. "Is it this?"

"No," he said, laughing quietly. "It's in the drawer."

He got up, and I heard plastic ripping, and then he was back. This time, he didn't have his pants on, and his warm legs tangled with mine again. We lay face to face, and he slipped a hand behind my head, drawing me in for a kiss while his other hand tugged my leg over his again. His fingers touched me first, and then his body touched me, pressing harder and harder until something in my body gave way, and I let him in. Pain clenched somewhere up inside me, and I gasped, tears springing to my eyes.

Jack stroked my hair back and kissed me softly. "Are you okay?"

In the moonlight, I could see his eyes shining with concern, his brow creased. He hadn't meant to hurt me, as my mother had said he would. It was an accident.

"Is that it?" I asked. "Did we do it?"

"No," he said. "I'm just waiting for you to get comfortable."

I ran my hands along his strong arms, his muscular back, his scratchy cheek. His skin was warm despite the cool night breeze sweeping in the window and washing over us like the moonlight. I breathed in the scent of him, gazing into his blue, anxious eyes. All around us, I could hear the breathing of the others, of my boys. This is what I'd wanted with them and not been able to name. I had finally absorbed one of them, drawn him into my body, claiming him as part of me.

In a minute, the painful tightness eased away, and Jack started to move against me. I could feel him inside me, the strangeness and wonder of it increasing as he moved, his lips pressing softly against mine, his strong arms cradling me like I was made entirely of treasure. And then it didn't feel strange but good, so good I had to bite my lip to keep from making a sound. I knew that no matter how long I lived, no matter how much treasure I made or spells I learned, I would never forget the magic of this moment.

Chapter Twenty-One

Astrid

I woke to find myself resting comfortably between two warm bodies. I nestled against them, relishing the smoothness of their skin against mine.

"Can I wake up like this every day?" William asked from one side.

"Not every day," Daniel said, sitting up in the far bed. "Sometimes I get to wake up like that."

Evan was nowhere to be seen.

"How long are we planning to hide a girl here?" Jack asked, propping up on one elbow to smile down at me. He leaned down and kissed my nose. "You good?"

"I'm good," I said, smiling up at him. I felt a strange shyness when our eyes met, as if being closer to him had made me more of a stranger instead of less.

"Hungry?" he asked.

"Famished."

Daniel ducked out of the room for a second before returning to report that their mother had gone to work. When we stepped out of the bedroom, an unearthly aroma of wonderfulness met us. It was smoky and salty and pure goodness. I sniffed my way along the hall, ignoring the chuckles of the guys. In the small kitchen we found Evan standing at the stove, his hair wet from the shower and dripping onto his shoulders. I didn't know if my mouth was watering from the salty, smoky smell or the sight of him standing there in a pair of sweatpants slung low on his hips. His broad shoulders and muscular back drew my eyes like the scent had drawn me to the kitchen.

"I got toast," Jack said, grabbing a loaf of bread and dropping slices into a square black box.

"I'm on juice duty," William said, grabbing cups from a cabinet. He opened the refrigerator and brought out a pitcher of purple liquid.

"I'll entertain and enlighten our guest," Daniel said, pulling out a chair and bowing, gesturing with one hand for me to sit.

"And set the table," Evan said without turning.

"I can do something," I said.

"No way," Daniel said. "You're the princess. We're just commoners."

As I looked around at my wonderful boys, I knew they were anything but common. Or maybe common was a good thing. Maybe deep down I was common, too. I knew in that moment that I would give up a crown, a throne, and all the treasure in the world to stay here with these common boys in their common shifter house.

Daniel set plates on the table, and a minute later, Evan set scrambled eggs and strips of curly red and white meat.

"This is what smells so good," I said.

"You've never had bacon?" Daniel asked, dropping a handful of forks onto the small, chipped table. The four of them gaped at me like I'd just said that I'd never seen the sky.

"And I thought sex would be the best thing we taught you," Jack said with a wink.

Before I could answer, a loud booming sound came from outside, and the house shook on its blocks.

"What was that?" William asked, his eyes wide. The others were all staring wide-eyed, too. We stared at the door, which opened to the left of the kitchen and the right of the sitting area. It flew open with a bang, then hung at an awkward angle.

My mother loomed in the doorway. "Well, well, well. What do we have here?"

"Mother Dear," I said, rising halfway from my chair. "How did you find me?"

"Oh, I wonder," she snarled. "Do you really think I'm too stupid to find you? Just because you're an imbecile doesn't mean that I am."

"Hey," Jack said. "That's not necessary."

"You!" Mother Dear swung around, pointing a trembling finger at him. "You dare to speak to me after defiling my daughter?"

"I didn't defile her," Jack said. "I—I love her." He turned to me, his eyes earnest. "I do, Astrid. I love you."

"Oh, Jack," I said, running around the table and throwing my arms around him. "I love you."

A high-pitched laugh shrieked through the room. "Oh, this is too pathetic," Mother Dear said, still tittering. "My dear child, you can't really believe this boy loves you."

I felt Jack's body against mine, as firm and sure as the earth that had greeted my feet when I finally braved my escape from this monster.

"He does," I said, releasing him and turning to face her. "They do."

Her eyes moved from one boy to the next as they joined me. Jack rested his hands on my hips, and William took my hand in his, giving it a reassuring squeeze. Daniel took my other hand, lacing his fingers with mine.

"We do," Evan said, stepping up beside Jack.

Mother Dear's eyes narrowed, her lip curled in disgust. "I guess what they say is true. The apple doesn't fall far from the tree."

"What apple?" I asked.

"You, you idiot," she said. "Even when it's plucked as nothing more than a bud, and raised far from this degradation and depravity, it's in your blood. You can't help what you are.

I guess I shouldn't expect more than to find you letting a bunch of dirty shifters take turns with you."

"I think that's enough," Jack said, his voice low and menacing, nothing like the boy of sunshine and dimples I'd become accustomed to.

"I'm a witch," I said to Mother Dear. "Don't I get a collective?"

"You're no witch," she said. "You're trailer trash just like the boys you picked. I guess I can't blame you for being attracted to the very type you came from. I had hoped I could do better, but you can't fight your nature, can you, Astrid?"

"You knew I was an eagle all that time," I said. "Didn't you? You just didn't want me to know, because then I might fly out of my prison."

"Prison?" She drew back, her pretty face indignant. "I gave you everything a girl could dream of. What more could you ask for?"

"Life," I whispered, her betrayal fresh all over again. All that time, all those years, she had known. She had held me in that tower when I could have flown free. She had lied, told me I'd never be myself again if I shifted into my true form.

"Life? I gave you life. I birthed you from a borrowed body, enduring the agony of childbirth for a daughter who wasn't even mine. One day, I'd hoped she would be grateful."

"What?" I gasped, clutching at the boys' hands to steady myself.

"You want the truth?" Mother Dear asked. "Fine, here's the truth. Your father is a very weak man, Astrid. He's hardly more than an animal even in human form. In his youth, before he met me and knew real love, he was a slave to the desires of the flesh. He fell under the spell of the worst sort of girl, a piece of white trash who spread her legs for whatever came her way. But all he saw was a tight young body, and he couldn't help himself. And that's where you came from."

"Where?" I asked, shaking my head in confusion.

"Oh, for goddess sakes," she said. "He got her pregnant, you dimwit. And because he has a tender heart, he believed he could save even a piece of trailer trash like her. So, he married her. Remember when I told you about his first wife who died of madness? That's—your—mother." She ground the words out through clenched teeth, staring at me with such hatred my insides seemed to liquify.

"I'm not your daughter?" I asked, too bewildered to think of anything else. For some reason, that betrayal hurt almost worse than the others. That's what I'd always been above all else, above even being a princess. Tears filled my eyes as I stared at this woman, this stranger.

"You're my daughter," she said. "I raised you, didn't I? I loved and protected and provided for you when no one else wanted you. And what do I get in return? A daughter determined to follow in that woman's tragic footsteps. Your birth mother was weak, too, though. I can't really blame you for being the way you are, coming from two such weak souls."

"My mother didn't want me," I whispered, swiping tears off my cheeks as they began to solidify.

"No," Mother Dear said. "She didn't. She was too busy pining after your father, who by then had realized his folly. He left her and married someone worthy of his position—the wolf princess. But he didn't love her. He only loved me, as I love him. Our love will transcend even death."

"Then why didn't he marry you?" I asked.

She strode forward, and her hand whipped out, stinging across my cheek. Tears burst from my eyes then, and I had to grab for them before the boys saw.

"Whoa," Jack said, reaching around me to grab Mother Dear's wrist. "I'd think before I touched this girl again."

Mother's eyes blazed with that otherworldly magic, and she yanked her hand upwards. Jack flew across the kitchen and slammed into the stove. The bacon pan went flying. Sizzling strips of bacon flew into the air, and hot oils splattered over the stove and the counters, the wall, the floor. Jack.

"Jack," I cried, but Mother Dear grabbed my shoulders.

But no, she wasn't my mother. She was Yvonne. I would never call her Mother Dear again.

"Did you not hear me, you imbecile?" Mother Dear demanded, shaking my shoulders. Daniel tried to pry her loose while his brothers ran to Jack. The oil behind us crackled, and flames licked up from the burner where the pan had been.

Mother kept speaking like she didn't see any of it. Her eyes were ferocious. "Love has nothing to do with marriage. Stop living in a fairytale. Marriage is about what advantage you can bring to the table—wealth, a name, a position. I didn't have any of that. But you do."

"That's what you've been preparing me for all my life?" I sniffled, gathering treasure in my hand until I thought it would spill out between my fingers. Smoke billowed from the stove, and the flame shot higher when William threw water on it.

"No, stupid girl. I have been preparing you to be a queen. I don't give a damn about your love life."

"Right," I said, my eyes suddenly feeling dry as dust. I watched as if far away as the flame caught the curtain, devouring it in one hungry suck. Yvonne wasn't my mother. She didn't care if I was loved or happy. She only wanted me to do her bidding, to live the life she'd always wanted but never had. "If I'm not your daughter, why didn't I live with Father Dear? At least I'm his child."

Mother Dear gave me a haughty stare. "Because he didn't want you," she said. "He never wanted you. No one wanted you, Astrid. He was done with your mother before you came along. He only claims the daughters he had with his second wife."

My eyes stung with the smoke, and tears began again, but my feet stayed planted to the floor. I swallowed hard, wishing I hadn't asked for the truth. This was more truth than I was prepared for. I couldn't deny it, though. Father Dear knew I was alive, had always known I was in that tower, and he'd never come to take me out. On occasion, he had come to visit me, but only when Mother Dear was there, and when she left, he had always gone with her. If he wanted me, he could have taken me to his home in the shifter valley long ago.

I didn't even know if Yvonne wanted me, or if any princess would do. I only knew of four people who wanted me for who I was, not what I was. Four boys who I wanted more than I wanted treasure or titles, more than I had wanted to make Mother Dear happy. She had never worried about my happiness, after all. But they had.

"We need to get out," Evan said, coughing on the smoke. He and William had given up on putting it out, and it was now rapidly devouring the walls.

They hauled Jack up, who hung limp between them.

"Not so fast," Yvonne said, an evil smile twisting her lips. The door banged shut behind her.

"What are you doing?" I cried. "You can't lock us in here. We'll die."

"Bravo," Yvonne said, slowly clapping her hands together. "At least, they'll die. We have magic, don't we, dear?"

"We—we do?" I asked. "If I'm not your daughter, then that means I'm not a witch."

"Look at that, it only took you five whole minutes to figure out that one simple fact. You're not as stupid as I thought."

"It's not her fault that you failed to teach her the most basic things in life," Daniel said. "That doesn't make her stupid. That makes you evil."

"Oh, he's so cute when he's angry," Yvonne said. "I can see why you chose him."

"Let us out," William said, yanking at the doorknob.

The room was stifling, the smoke blurring my vision. Tears dribbled from my eyes, these ones brought on by the smoke. The window was right behind the fire, and the others were too small to provide any relief, though they were open. If anything, the draft coming in the lone window in the sitting room was making the flames move faster.

"This trailer isn't meant for fire," William shouted. "We're going to cook in here in under a minute."

"Let them out," I yelled at Yvonne, forgetting all about our quarrel. What mattered was getting the boys out.

"I might," Yvonne said. "If you go back to the tower where you belong and wait for your day in the sun like you were supposed to. You got greedy, though, and now your boys will pay."

"Go out the bedroom window," I said to Daniel, slipping my hand in his pocket and opening it, spilling a fistful of gold.

182

"Not without you," he said. "No way are we leaving you."

"Go," I yelled, but when I turned, my heart nearly stopped. The flames had filled the entrance to the hallway, racing down the walls. We didn't have even a minute.

"Okay," I said to Yvonne, grabbing her arm. "I'll do whatever you want. Just let them out."

"Just let them out?" Yvonne asked. "Now why would I do that?"

"Please," I said. "I'll never see them again. I promise."

"No," Evan yelled.

"It's worth it if it means you can live," I said, tears streaming off my face. I didn't bother to catch them. What was treasure to a dead girl?

Pieces of plaster and wallpaper fluttered down like the flaming bodies of birds. Like the chance of freedom that my own flame-colored falcon had offered. That dream was dead. And if these boys died, if they were hurt, I'd die with them. Alone in my tower, I might look perfectly safe, but there would be no life left inside me. I would be like one of the shells Yvonne brought home, the lifeless bodies who she animated through her sorcery, through projecting herself into them.

I had been such a fool to think I could run, to think I could escape her. I had been naïve, so excited about leaving that I hadn't even considered what she'd do when she caught up. I had known somewhere deep down that she would find me and bring me back.

Before then, I'd meant to get answers, to see the world I'd never been a part of. But I had thought I'd have more time, that I'd have a taste of freedom and then go home. I hadn't considered what she would do to exact revenge, what punishment she would dole out for my insurrection. Of course she would want some revenge, some guarantee that I would never betray her again.

"I'm sorry," I said, grasping at Yvonne. I threw my arms around her, clinging to her neck. "You were right. Their world is awful. Their house is a dump that deserves to burn. Please forgive me. Take me home, Mother Dear. I'll never leave my room without permission again."

The door flew open, and Evan threw William out. Daniel leapt out after him, rolling across the ground.

"Come on," Evan said.

"No," Jack cried, staggering toward me, a goose-egg knot on his forehead from where he'd hit the stove. His shirt was on fire, his eyes streaming tears. I knew now that I could never escape. And worse than that, if I refused to go back to the tower, the boys would never escape. They would never be safe as long as she knew I loved them.

"Go away," I screamed at Jack. "I don't love you. I only wanted someone to take me away. I don't care about you. I don't want you. Now get away from me." I cowered against Mother Dear, turning my face away when I couldn't bear to see the look on his face, like it was shattering before my eyes.

"Listen to the girl," Yvonne said, holding up a hand. A streak of lightning shot from her palm, searing into Jack's face. He screamed, clutching his face and stumbling backward. Evan tackled him and dove for the door just as the ceiling caved in. With a whoosh, the house went up like a fireball.

Chapter Twenty-Two

Astrid

A row of candles flickered in front of the mirror, their wax making misshapen, deformed figures. Inside the frame, two faces blinked back, one above the other. "A queen must always look the part," Mother Dear said, standing behind my chair as she ran a comb through my hair. "Her long, flowing locks are one of her greatest assets."

"Yes, Mother Dear," I said.

"Which is why you shouldn't have them right now," she said. "It will be a while yet before you are ready to be a queen. First, you must prove yourself a worthy princess, and a worthy opponent to your sisters."

"That's right," I said. "My evil sisters." I barely felt the stroke of her machete-sized knife as she set down the comb and began to saw at my hair.

"Sisters who want you alive even less than your father," Mother Dear reminded me. "They are the girls who will usurp your throne. They are the girls who would have you killed if they could. Despite your unsavory beginnings, you are the true heir, Astrid. You are the princess. That's why I have kept you safely hidden all these years. When he no longer wants to rule, the shifters will recognize you, the child of his first wife. But if the daughters of his second wife have their way, you'll never get that chance."

I mulled that over. "You said one of them wants to marry the wolf prince?"

"Yes."

"Why don't we make a trade?" I said. "She gets the wolf prince, and I get the shifter crown. Then we can all get what we want."

Mother Dear gave me a long look, one I'd never seen on her face before. One that said maybe I was more than she'd given me credit for. I couldn't tell if she was proud or wary of me. I didn't want her to think I was a worthy opponent of her, though. One day, I would be free. Until then, I had to play along.

"Right now, the prince isn't as desirable as you imagine," she said. "He's quite hideous, in fact. But even still, I don't think your sister will agree to such an arrangement. She's stubborn and greedy. I have tried to reason with her, but she refuses to listen. She wants it all."

I didn't want any of it, but maybe if I went along with Mother Dear and accepted her word, I would live. Better still, my boys would live. Until then, I could only hope that they knew I hadn't meant what I'd had to say. I had given them the treasure, but it killed me that I couldn't do more, that I couldn't see them again and make sure that they were okay.

"I'm working on getting him out of the picture," Mother Dear was saying. "If I can find a way to gain control of the Second Valley, and you have control of the Third, we'll be an unstoppable team."

She stepped back and smiled at me in the mirror. I stared at my hair, the burned bits gone, the remaining length chopped to just around my ears. Mother Dear had cast a protection spell around us in the fire, but she'd let my hair burn, let me feel a shadow of what a real burn would feel like. But I didn't care about my hair, or treasure, or looking like a queen. I didn't even care about being queen.

I would do it to please Mother Dear for now. When I was queen, I could help the boys. I could help everyone in the valley who lived in a house no bigger than a box and slept on a couch. Even if I could never marry the boys, I could give them a better life, the way they'd given me a better life for a while.

And maybe by then I would have found a way to rid myself of Mother's control. Maybe, when I was queen, I could make the rules.

"We've got that chopped," Mother Dear said. "Now it's time for you to chop the vines."

NO!

I balled my fists, wanting to scream, to rip out her hair, to take her giant machete-knife and chop off her head. I wanted to tell her I'd die before I'd cut down the vines that had brought me the boys, that had given me companionship and company as I sang to them each day, that had given me hope.

Instead, I nodded and cast my eyes down, as I always had. "Yes, Mother Dear."

She threw open the shutters that she'd brought to cover the windows. I knew they were more than the wood that made them up. They had magic, a protection spell, something to keep me from opening them.

"Good girl," she said. "The better you are, the more privileges you can earn back. One day, I might even open the windows. For now, enjoy the sun while we're outside."

"You're never going to let me out again, are you?" I asked.

"Maybe one day," she said, clucking her tongue. "For now, you have no reason to leave." I lowered her down on the rope, hoping that somehow it would break halfway down. Wishing that I could drop her and know she'd die.

I shifted into a raven this time, fluttering down to join her. At least she hadn't taken my shifting away from me. As I descended, I fought the urge to fly away, down the mountain and over the next one, into the shifter valley where I belonged. If I did, though, she would follow me. She would hurt my boys. And I couldn't let that happen. As long as she lived, I would never be free. She would never let me go.

I had to be patient. One day, my moment would come. Not my moment to take the throne, but my moment to take back my life. But I had to be patient, to wait for the moment when I could get rid of her once and for all. That was okay. I was a patient girl. I'd spent my whole life waiting for her dreams to come true. Now I was waiting for my own.

Mother Dear handed me the knife, and I knelt at the base of the vines. I began to chop at them, my eyes blurring with tears. The sap was like blood spilling on the ground, blood on the knife, blood on my hands.

"I'm sorry," I whispered, letting the golden teardrops fall from my eyes.

When it was done, I handed Mother Dear the knife. I knew the vine was truly dead this time, that I had cut through every last one of its stems. I knew it was dead because it didn't feel like my friend anymore. It didn't give me hope anymore. And I didn't feel sad anymore. I felt nothing as I shifted into a bird and flew back into my cage.

Chapter Twenty-Three

Jack

"Just a little further," I said.

"Okay, but only a few more minutes," Daniel said, gripping my elbow. He may have been the dog, but I was doggedly determined. Every day I walked in the woods, feeling the sun on my face, trying to learn the scents and sensations of a tree in my path, the signs underfoot that meant I was nearing a stream or a cliff's edge. One day, I would walk alone again.

It had been three months, and we hadn't heard a word from her. We'd used the gift she'd given us to get our mother a new house. It was just a small, simple one. That's all she'd wanted. We still shared a bedroom, but that was by choice. Now Mom had her own room, too. And we still had some gold in a safe for when things got tight, our payment for being the princess's guides.

When I'd stolen the witch's wedding gift, I'd hoped to find diamonds in that package. I'd found seeds instead. Those seeds had led me to treasure, even if it wasn't diamonds. But Astrid's treasure was different, earned through pain.

The real treasure hadn't been the gold, though. It had been her.

Mom said it wasn't worth losing my vision, but I wasn't so sure. One night with Astrid seemed worth anything to me.

I hadn't believed her words at first. I had thought the gift meant something, that maybe she was coming back. I imagined her sitting on her windowsill combing out her long hair, letting it fall ten feet down the wall of the tower. I imagined her watching the leaves turn from spring green to the deep forest green of summer to the gold and orange of autumn. I had felt the signs of autumn in the air even if I couldn't see them.

"Did you hear that?" I asked, cocking my head.

"What?" William asked.

The four of us halted, and the crunch of leaves underfoot died away.

"You didn't hear it?" I asked.

"It would help to know what I'm listening for," Daniel said.

And then it came again, the clear sweet note of her voice. "It's her," I choked out.

Daniel didn't answer. For a second, I thought maybe he'd run ahead to find her. But I would have heard him move. He was frozen like me, listening in silent awe to that voice, like an angel on high. Literally.

"Then she's alive," Evan said at last.

"Yeah." I was glad, of course, even knowing what it meant. We'd all gone up to the tower after she left. Even I had gone, insisting they take me up, that I could convince her to open the window or come down. But she'd never answered, even when William turned into a bird and beat himself against her shutters. For all we knew, she was as dead as our beanstalk.

But now we knew. She was still alive, still singing. We'd thought maybe she'd come back, just as we'd hoped maybe my eyesight would. But I remained blind as a result of the witch's lightning fingers, and Astrid remained elusive, gone from our lives.

Still, that song. That voice.

"She sounds happy," William said after a while.

I was happy that she was singing. I was happy to hear her voice, even if that was the only piece of her I ever got. It wasn't enough, not even close to enough, but I would take it. I would take her happiness, the joy in her song, and I would find my own happiness in it.

I raised my blind eyes to the sun, and I smiled.

Chapter Twenty-Four

Astrid

The leaves were falling by the time Mother Dear let me see the sun again. For a few days, she stayed close, but not for long. She was busy in the wolf valley, carving out a place for herself among the wolves. It wasn't enough for her to have a place in the coven. She needed more. She would always need more.

I didn't need more. I had found what I was looking for. So when Mother Dear went off for a few days, I knew we were back to our old routines. I had proven myself, had earned her trust. It hadn't been easy—I had bitten my tongue so many times I was surprised I had a tongue left at all.

I perched on the windowsill, looking out over the mountains for a minute, and then I let myself fall. I wasn't scared this time. For months, I'd had nothing to do but shift and practice flying. I could shift in seconds, and landing was no longer a problem.

I soared down the mountain, knowing that I would find my way to the boys, that my heart would lead me like a compass. The shifter valley was big, but I knew the way. Soon enough, I had come upon a little blue house with white shutters where the trailer had stood. The only signs of it were the bits of blackened earth visible at the edges. I heard voices, and I flew around back. A small fence surrounded a little plot of earth where four boys were digging. I sat on the fence post, watching them work, and I sang them a song.

Evan had his shirt off despite the slight chill of autumn in the air, collecting more freckles on his shoulders. He was digging hard with a fork while Jack dug in the dirt at his feet. A row of dirty, orange potatoes lay where they had already dug. Daniel was yanking vines back ahead of them while William chopped at their stems. None of them looked my way, even when I sang. My heart sank. Didn't they know I was coming back?

I flew to the ground at the end of the row. Still, no one paid me any mind. I shifted into human form. That got their attention.

They all stopped working and stared at me except Jack. He kept digging like nothing had happened.

I walked over, stepping over the row and kneeling beside Jack. Wordlessly, I began to dig.

"What are you doing?" he asked.

"A queen should be in touch with her people," I said.

Jack's hands went still, and he turned toward me. He wore a pair of sunglasses, so I couldn't see his eyes as he looked at me, remaining perfectly still as he took me in. Then he slipped his hand from his glove and reached out, laying his fingertips on my cheek. Warmth swept through my body, and I sighed at his touch. His fingers ran over my skin, finding my jawline, my chin, my lips. I pressed a kiss to his fingertips before he slid them away, over my nose and eyelids, my temples, then ran his hand over my head, down my back where my hair lay. It was only down to my waist now, growing faster each day.

"It's really you," he said.

"He can't see," Daniel said.

"With my eyes," Jack said with a small smile. "I see with my hands now."

Tears filled my eyes, and I let them drop. "I'm sorry," I whispered.

Jack cupped the back of my head, pulling me in until our foreheads rested together.

"Thank you," Evan said, resting a foot on his digging fork.

"For what?" I asked, raising my face to his.

He shrugged and cut his eyes toward the house.

I looked down, picking tears off the ground. "There's more," I said.

"I know," Daniel reminded me with his same big grin as always. "I told them, too, so they know. But they don't really know. It's hard to believe without seeing it."

"Thanks," Jack said, tossing a scrawny potato at him.

William held out a hand, and I took it, that same wash of shyness coming over me that I'd felt the morning I'd woken up here. He pulled me to my feet, wrapping me in a tight embrace. For a long minute, we stood without moving, without speaking. Finally, he released me.

"How long are you here?"

"A few hours," I said.

"That's it?" Evan said, and though his voice was flat, I saw the anguish in his eyes.

"It's what I can risk," I said. "I can't have her coming after you again."

"Totally worth it," William said.

Daniel pulled me to him and planted a hard kiss on my lips. Then he grinned and wiggled his eyebrows. "We can do a lot in a few hours."

Evan shoved the fork into the ground and started digging again. Hurt flickered through me that he wasn't going to embrace me as the others had. But I had time to win him back. I knelt at the foot of the fork and began to dig in the dirt with Jack.

"You're getting your hands dirty there, princess," Evan said.

"That's okay," I said. "I bet you still have a shower."

William gulped, his eyes widening. He obviously hadn't forgotten me.

"Is this like a one-time thing?" Jack asked. "Or how often does a queen mingle with commoners?"

"Y'all sound like a bunch of girls," Daniel said. "Where is this going? I need you to define our relationship right now."

William punched his shoulder, and they started shoving each other around.

I turned to Jack. "I figure a queen should get out among her people at least a few times a week."

"And how does your mother feel about that?"

"A princess should sneak out of her tower a few times a week, too," I said, unearthing a fat orange potato.

A slow smile spread across Jack's face as he dug his hands into the dirt beside mine.

"Besides," I said. "I was promised bacon."

From the Author

Hey, y'all!

I hope you enjoyed this twisted tale! At the end of last year, I asked my readers what they wanted to see. The majority wanted paranormal RH with a little more steam and a lot of grit before a hopefully-ever-after. I hope this one delivered!

I weigh my projects based on how many people are clamoring for the next book, so if you're wanting more, don't forget to let me know by leaving a review.

Also by Lena Mae Hill

Want more gritty fairytales set in the Three Valleys?
It all starts in the <u>Complete Girl Among Wolves Trilogy:</u>
Unlikely Magic
Beastly Beauty
Ghostly Snow

Want more RH fairytales? Or to know what's up with the girl who flew into Astrid's room that first day? Find out in *Twisted*.

Want more RH mythology, or to know about Astrid's golden tears? Read the <u>Complete Hosting Gods Trilogy</u>:
Emerge
Ignite
Ascend

Want to find out about Mother Dear? Start her story in the <u>Winslow Witch Chronicles</u> (series in progress).

CAGED

Magic of the Void
Sister of the Sea
Witch of the Wind (coming 2019)